D0428904

GRAEME SIMSION is the internationally bestselling author of *The Rosie Project*, *The Rosie Effect*, and *The Rosie Result*, featuring Professor Don Tillman, as well as *The Best of Adam Sharp* and—with his wife, Anne Buist—*Two Steps Forward*. He is based in Melbourne.

DON TILLMAN'S STANDARDIZED MEAL SYSTEM

Recipes & tips from
the star of the *Rosie* novels

GRAEME SIMSION

TEXT PUBLISHING MELBOURNE AUSTRALIA

textpublishing.com.au

The Text Publishing Company
Swann House, 22 William Street, Melbourne Victoria 3000, Australia

Copyright © Graeme Simsion, 2019

The moral right of Graeme Simsion to be identified as the author of this work has been asserted.

Published by The Text Publishing Company, 2019

Book design by W. H. Chong
Typeset by J&M Typesetting & Text

Printed and bound in Australia by Griffin Press, part of Ovato, an accredited ISO/NZS 14001:2004 Environmental Management System printer

ISBN: 9781922268167 (hardback)
ISBN: 9781925774931 (ebook)

A catalogue record for this book is available from the National Library of Australia

This book is printed on paper certified against the Forest Stewardship Council® Standards. Griffin Press holds FSC chain-of-custody certification SGS-COC-005088. FSC promotes environmentally responsible, socially beneficial and economically viable management of the world's forests.

Contents

Rationale

"So, you cook this same meal every Tuesday, right?"

"Correct." I listed the eight major advantages of the Standardized Meal System.

1. No need to accumulate recipe books.

2. Standard shopping list — hence very efficient shopping.

3. Almost zero waste — nothing in the refrigerator or pantry unless required for one of the recipes.

4. Diet planned and nutritionally balanced in advance.

5. No time wasted wondering what to cook.

6. No mistakes, no unpleasant surprises.

7. Excellent food, superior to most restaurants at a much lower price (see point 3).

8. Minimal cognitive load required.

On my first date with Rosie Jarman, the woman who would, incredibly, become my (remainder of) life partner, I was unsure of her retention capabilities and selected the number of items according to Miller's (1956) "seven plus or minus two" rule. Had I known she was at the high end of neurotypical memory function, I would have added:

9. Rationalization of kitchen equipment — no cupboards and drawers full of items that are "hardly ever used." The financial savings allow me to own

a smaller set of high-quality cooking tools and invest in leading-edge barbecue technology.

10. Ability to optimize recipes, quantities, and cooking times through continuous feedback.

I would *not* have added "Improved mental health through reduced anxiety and the comfort of routine," as I was not conscious of that benefit at the time.

Nor was I aware of the *disadvantages* of the Standardized Meal System. Rosie and our son, Hudson, filled that gap in my knowledge. The problems included (note past tense):

1. Failure to accommodate a partner who did not want to eat lobster every Tuesday. After my first attempt at rectifying the problem, Rosie clarified that this quite clear and specific statement was to be interpreted as not wanting *any* immutable meal assigned to *any* day of the week, and "certainly not forever."

2. No allowance for partner's, child's, or guests' food preferences, allergies, or ethical restrictions.

3. Perception of the Standardized Meal System as a symptom of rigidity rather than efficiency.

4. Inability to expose a child (or adult) to a wide variety of foods.

5. No allowance for random, short-notice decisions by partner to invite guests or eat out.

6. No contingency plan in the event of disasters such as unavailability of a key ingredient, child-related crisis, or university meeting scheduled during time allocated for shopping or cooking.

7. No process for ongoing evolution of the system.

All problems have now been solved. In the case of item 3, no change to the system was required; instead, I stopped worrying about what unrelated people thought of me. Virtually all meals now allow for variants; no meal is current for more than thirteen weeks (a season); emergencies and dining out are explicitly catered for; and there is provision for both incremental improvement and the introduction of new meals.

Also, since the publication of the three *Rosie* memoirs, multiple people have contacted me, not to call me rigid or boring or obsessive, but seeking details of how to implement the Standardized Meal System. Hence this book, applying thirty-six years of experience and feedback to what was already an excellent design.

I recommend this fully revised Standardized Meal System as a tool for modifying the behavior of people who irrationally and compulsively devote unnecessary resources to food shopping, meal design, and cooking, with consequent negative impact on their performance in social, occupational, or other important areas.

Principles and Rules

The principles behind the Standardized Meal System are simple:

1. A standard menu for each week of each season (I recommend commencing on the Saturday closest to the first day of the season).

2. Lunches not specified, except for Saturdays. Weekday lunches are purchased at work or sourced from deliberate creation of leftovers. Sunday brunch is eaten at a cafe or replaced by a late breakfast.

3. Consistent breakfast throughout the year (with seasonal fruit adjustments).

4. Recipes (except for guest nights — refer item 7) are for two people but readily scaled up or down (number chosen to facilitate scaling calculations for people who are incompetent at mental arithmetic).

5. Two shopping expeditions (Tuesday and Saturday) each week, using standardized shopping lists for each season.

6. Common Resources (e.g. salt, lemons, tequila) purchased in economic quantities and added to the shopping list when the last container is opened or the quantity remaining is insufficient for the next meal. Purchases can be made at other times to take advantage of discounts.

7. Tuesday is guest night. Recipes allow for four people, i.e. two guests (optimum). A weekday is nominated,

as invitees are less likely to have conflicting dining-out commitments and it supports the social convention of announcing "It's a school night" when you want guests to leave.

8. Friday is restaurant night. An alternative (typically frozen) meal is available as backup if you decide to eat at home. These backup meals can also be used in emergencies.

9. Sunday is the major cooking day for replenishing resources such as chicken stock and frozen meals, and preparing for the week ahead.

10. Alcohol is specified on Saturday, Tuesday, and Friday nights. If you don't drink alcohol or want to drink less (or more[1]), this is easily varied.

11. The menus and schedule should be seen as a starting point for tailoring to include your own dietary rules, food preferences, and quantities.

---

[1] I do not recommend drinking more. I do not *recommend* drinking alcohol at all.

General Advice

1. *Very important:* the adjective "approximately" can be inserted into all recipes, wherever it will reduce effort and stress. I incurred incredible amounts of both before learning this fact, which applies to sizes, shapes[1], quantities, and timings. Precision is necessary only in baking (bread, biscuits, cakes — which do not feature in this book, with the exception of gougères on Winter Tuesday). Otherwise, variation of 20%, and even the omission of one or two ingredients not included in the name of the recipe, is almost always acceptable.

   Conversely, if there are obvious signs that a temperature or process time should be varied (e.g. items burning, boiling over, exploding[2]), rectification of the problem should take precedence over adhering to the recipe and the instructions should be modified for future use.

2. Virtually all cooking requires a general-purpose "kitchen" knife, wooden spoon, spatula, chopping board, vegetable peeler, plastic cling wrap, paper towels, scales, measuring spoons, and measuring jug. Many recipes require cooking oil, olive oil, salt, and pepper. I also recommend use of an apron and onion-peeling goggles, the latter with prescription

---

[1] It is impossible to cut an irregularly shaped vegetable (i.e. any vegetable) into cubes, for example.

[2] I have only had explosion problems in the case of chestnuts (refer *The Rosie Result*), which are not used in this book.

lenses if you wear glasses. These items should be stored where they can be easily accessed, and are not listed under the specific equipment and ingredients for each recipe.

If you are using a barbecue (highly recommended), I suggest keeping a second set of items at that location, as well as a barbecue spatula and tongs.

3. Assemble ingredients and equipment before commencing cooking.

4. A timer is essential. Use it whenever there is substantial time between steps, particularly if food is left to cool before refrigerating (easily forgotten while bacteria multiply). I use my smart watch under voice command.

5. I have provided detailed timings (in minutes, in the left column of the Process section) only when I consider them likely to be helpful. *All times are approximate:* if you become anxious, ignore all but the cooking durations. A dinner served late or early is not a disaster, and the problem will disappear as you become familiar with the process through weekly repetition.

6. Most meals are designed to be served on shared "central" plates, from which diners can take the amount that they want. This improves diner autonomy and eliminates "plating" effort. An examination of leftovers will assist in tuning quantities for the future.

7. I recommend always having salt, pepper, and a chili-based condiment on the table, to allow diners to add the quantities they prefer. Published recipes frequently suggest adding salt and pepper "to taste," implicitly acknowledging that tastes vary but allowing

the chef's taste to override those of other diners. In my experience, *most diners will want to add salt* (the spaghetti puttanesca is a notable exception).

8. I recommend becoming a regular customer of specialist vendors: greengrocer, delicatessen, baker, butcher, fishmonger. Your loyalty will prompt high-quality service and satisfying social interactions, with consequent benefits to your — and their — mental health.

9. I make extensive use of the barbecue (more accurately, *barbecues*), but the translation to burner / hotplate, grill, or oven is simple and obvious. Instructions are for a gas barbecue, but equivalent (and often better) results can be achieved with a charcoal-burning device. Once you are familiar with the operation of your barbecue, translation is again simple and obvious.

10. Some Common Resources items are most economically obtained from supermarkets, which I find noisy and unpleasant. If you have a housemate, I suggest they take responsibility for *all* supermarket shopping.

11. I have not included individual cutlery, serving implements, or plates in my equipment lists. If you have housemates, I recommend you delegate one to set the table and clean up in (partial) exchange for you taking responsibility for cooking and most of the shopping.

12. You should not refuse offers by other household members to cook. I suggest Friday, when they can prepare the meal as an alternative to restaurant dining. The stress levels are likely to be even higher, but alcohol is permitted on Fridays. If they want

to contribute more frequently, they should participate in the Standardized Meal System.

13. I am Australian, hence accustomed to American reviewers of my publications pointing out "spelling errors." The reverse (as I discovered during my time in the US) does not seem to happen to American academics. To avoid being considered sloppy or unfamiliar with English, I now write my papers in American English and have adopted this practice here, along with the Oxford comma, which I am in favor of in any case. However, I have retained Australian usages such as "minced beef," "coriander" (in reference to leaves), and "autumn" in the hope that they will encourage greater awareness of language differences and appreciation / understanding of non-American cultures.

14. As a scientist, I use the metric system. In this book, I have supplemented it with universal cooking measures: spoons and cups. If you are accustomed to imperial measures, I recommend purchasing a set of metric scales, and small and large liquid measures — a relatively small investment and more convenient than referring to conversion tables[1]. All temperatures in this book are degrees Celsius. You can convert mentally (recommended) using the simple formula Degrees (Fahrenheit) = Degrees (Celsius) x 1.8 + 32. Alternatively, you can memorise conversions for the few commonly used temperatures, replace the barbecue thermometer, and / or note the conversions on your kitchen whiteboard.

---

[1] Conversion tables are of course widely available; if you prefer this option, you can download one. Better, memorize the conversion rates and calculate mentally. There is some evidence that brain exercise of this kind may slow the onset of dementia.

Breakfast

Research on the criticality of breakfast is inconclusive, as is much research on nutrition.

In formulating the Standardized Meal System, I was overwhelmed with dietary advice, much of it unscientific, contradictory, or exaggerated in terms of its potential benefits. It became obvious that my original goal of making the system nutritionally perfect, based on universally accepted research, was not feasible.

Instead, I identified five principles likely to provide a high proportion of the health benefits available from food choices[1]. Obviously, if you are (probably irrationally) convinced of the benefits of some "superfood" item or category, you will tailor the system to accommodate it. It is unlikely your health or weight will be significantly affected[2].

The principles are:

1. No junk food.

2. A variety of fruit and vegetables every day.

---

[1] I am not a professional dietician and you should not rely on my advice. But you should trust it more than that of unqualified authors of diet books and journalists reporting research. Or anyone suggesting that diet replace medicine.

[2] If you are concerned about health: do not smoke, exercise regularly, maintain a healthy BMI, and pay attention to the quality of your relationships (preferably with a live-in companion who can provide emotional support and take action in case of accident or illness: this companion will be motivated to stay to enjoy your cooking). Statistically, these strategies are more effective than any extensions to my diet principles.

3. Red meat once or twice a week, with remaining meals based on poultry, seafood, and / or vegetables.

4. No alcohol (strongly recommended but ignored in my case).

5. No rigid rules (hence, ice-cream is permitted on Autumn Sundays and chocolates once a week).

I decided to eat breakfast regularly because it provides a consistent start to the day; is a useful vehicle for delivering fruit, fiber, and caffeine; and reduces the impact of missing lunch if I become occupied with an interesting task.

I eat the same generic breakfast *every day, all year, potentially forever*, only varying the fruit component. I receive no criticism for this. People who consider the repetition of a dinner after an interval of seven days to be "boring" or even indicative of mental illness are prepared to eat the same breakfast after a delay of only twenty-four hours.

My original breakfast consisted of uncooked oats, to which I added dried fruit and nuts, plus fresh fruit. Rosie added yogurt to hers. I didn't, due to not liking yogurt. I have now upgraded to granola, using largely the same ingredients, but with the addition of a toasting process. It has three major advantages:

1. Assembly (excluding the fresh fruit) is done in bulk, in advance, in a relaxing context.

2. By formalizing the recipe, consistency is improved and ongoing refinement is more easily managed.

3. Superior flavor.

The average number of serves from the specified quantity is 71, i.e. 35 1/2 breakfasts for two people.

Granola production can be undertaken at any time, though Sunday is the obvious choice.

COMMON RESOURCES: GRANOLA

4 tbsp vegetable oil
300 g pepitas
750 g oats
60 g brown flaxseed
400 g pecans
750 g almonds
1 tsp nutmeg
1 tsp cinnamon
4 tbsp honey
2 tsp vanilla essence
250 g Turkish dried apricots
300 g dried cranberries ("craisins") — dried cherries
    are superior but more expensive

EQUIPMENT: GRANOLA

3 sheets baking paper
3 oven trays
Large bowl
Airtight jars for storage
Food processor

PROCESS: GRANOLA

Time: 68 minutes.

Preheat oven to 175 degrees and cover 3 oven trays with baking paper.

Put almonds and pecans in the food processor, and use chop mode briefly to halve size. Or chop manually.

Chop each dried apricot into 8 pieces.

Mix all ingredients except dried fruit together in a bowl.

Spread 1/3 of bowl contents onto each of the 3 oven trays.

If you are confident that the temperature of your oven is uniform across 3 shelves, you can use 3 oven trays concurrently, thus saving 32 minutes, minimum. But many ovens produce different temperatures at different levels and depending on what shelves are in use, creating a *nightmare*.

Ideally, you would purchase an oven without this problem, saving at least 5 hours and 29 minutes per year. If you are, for other reasons, replacing your oven, you could insist on a granola test. But I would not recommend replacement for this reason alone. The 5 hours and 29 minutes is not wasted if you time-share other tasks, including unstructured reflection, and the money (in my opinion) would be better served in expanding barbecue options. Most of my oven use is simple, and a superior appliance will make minimal difference to the result.

Put first tray in the oven — commence timing.

After 8 minutes, stir the ingredients, bringing in those on the sides as these are susceptible to burning.

After 16 minutes, remove tray from oven.

Repeat for remaining trays.

Immediately after removing a tray from the oven, add 1/3 of the dried fruit and stir to create a homogenous mix.

Allow to cool and store in jar(s) in the pantry.

COMMON RESOURCES: BREAKFAST

Fresh fruit (I recommend berries, stone fruit, oranges, apples, bananas)

Yogurt or other dairy product or substitute (optional)

Coffee

PROCESS: BREAKFAST

Time: 3 minutes.

Put granola in bowl.

Prepare fruit for eating (peel; cut into pieces; remove stones as necessary).

Add fruit and (optionally) dairy product or substitute to bowl.

Accompany with coffee (or alternative preferred beverage).

SPRING

SATURDAY
Lunch
Omelet with herbs and green salad

Dinner
Grilled asparagus
Beer-can chicken with roast vegetables

SUNDAY
Barbecued flounder with steamed vegetables
Mango sorbet

MONDAY
Chicken and roast-vegetable salad

TUESDAY
(guests)
Chorizo dates
Chermoula-spiced salmon with couscous
Turkish delight

WEDNESDAY
Mushroom risotto with green salad
Chocolates

THURSDAY
Tacos with salmon and guacamole

FRIDAY
(if eating at home)
Pizza

Omelet with Herbs and Green Salad

Omelets are one of the world's most flexible foods: acceptable for any meal, even emergency late-night supper if dinner has been delayed (incredibly, parent—teacher nights and public lectures are frequently scheduled during dinner time). Fillings can be changed to use leftovers and provide variety, which is important to some people.

On a Saturday, there is the possibility that the daily schedule will be disrupted by sleeping in and related activities, even to the extent of omitting breakfast. The omelet can then be served for "brunch." A familiar meal will help to restore order.

If this is the first time you have made an omelet (or if previous attempts have been unsuccessful), I recommend googling[1] the task and studying one or more videos. The procedure is simple but better communicated visually. Appearance improves with practice; however, the results are seldom inedible.

By the end of your first spring using the Standardized Meal System, you will be an expert, with a useful and portable life skill. Almost everyone has the ingredients for an omelet, but many lack a non-stick pan — more specifically, a non-stick pan which has not lost its non-stick properties through use of an unsuitable spatula or cleaning regimen. If your host has a

---

[1] You can use whatever search engine you prefer; a search on YouTube is likely to be quicker in this case. However, only Google has attained the ubiquity needed to acquire a verb form, and I was under editorial pressure to keep all instructions as concise as possible, despite my repeated warnings about the risk of ambiguity and confusion.

damaged non-stick pan, I recommend disposing of it — surreptitiously, because experience suggests they will react negatively to advice on the importance of proper maintenance[1].

COMMON RESOURCES: OMELET

4 eggs
1 tbsp milk
1 tbsp butter

RECIPE-SPECIFIC INGREDIENTS: OMELET

1 or 2 varieties of herb (I recommend French tarragon and you will have basil for the salad)

COMMON RESOURCES: SALAD

1 tbsp red-wine vinegar

RECIPE-SPECIFIC INGREDIENTS: SALAD

8 basil leaves
70 g salad greens

EQUIPMENT

Non-stick frying pan (20 cm diameter)
Bowl
Whisk or fork
Salad bowl
Salad servers
Jar for vinaigrette-making

---

[1] The majority of humans (not including myself) react negatively to unsolicited advice. The *advice* "don't give advice unless it's asked for" is patently flawed: people frequently don't realize that they need advice.

PROCESS

Time: 12 minutes.

Check: ensure you have made an omelet previously or watched instructional video.

Chop omelet herbs into pieces (1/2 cm square[1]) to produce 2 tablespoons of each chopped herb.

Put leaves in salad bowl. Tear basil leaves from stalks and add to salad bowl.

Put vinegar and 3 tablespoons of olive oil in jar with 1/4 teaspoon of salt. Put lid on jar (important) and shake vigorously for 15 seconds.

Pour contents of jar on salad and mix with salad servers.

Put pan on burner / hotplate, add butter, and set to 75% of maximum heat.

Break eggs into bowl, add milk and salt, and whisk with whisk or fork until frothy (1 minute).

Add chopped herbs, stir, then pour contents into pan.

Perform omelet–cooking procedure (6 minutes).

Remove omelet to a plate, cut in half, and put half on second plate.

VARIATIONS

Vary herb choice and combinations.

Add grated cheese, smoked salmon, chopped tomatoes, or pre–fried bacon / mushrooms / chorizo to omelet as soon as the base is firm enough to support them. You can omit the herb(s).

---

[1] First reminder: *approximately.*

SPRING SATURDAY DINNER:

Grilled Asparagus;
Beer–can Chicken with Roast Vegetables

Recommended alcohol: wine surplus to cooking process. White wine is probably preferable for cooking, but I prefer red for drinking. Almost any wine is compatible with chicken.

In restaurants it is conventional to order, in addition to the main course, a first course and / or dessert. Even my mother, who did not meet any of the criteria for classification as a "foodie," always made dessert and sometimes soup. However, in researching this book, I was amazed to discover that my friends and colleagues routinely cook only a single course[1].

To accommodate this practice, I have "dumbed down" the Standardized Meal System to specify only one course on some days. However, tonight's meal is an excellent example of the advantages of multiple courses. The chicken requires considerable time to cook, and the resulting smells will stimulate appetites, create impatience, and possibly provoke alcohol consumption. It is generally recommended that alcohol be accompanied by food.

The asparagus takes advantage of the barbecue being in operation. A green vegetable should accompany the chicken, and there is zero net increase in effort in cooking the two items serially rather than in parallel. Coordination of cooking times is also simplified.

---

[1] Amazed because, when I had dined at their homes, they had served more than one course — but only because I was present. A classic example of the presence of the researcher influencing the behavior under investigation (the Hawthorne effect, in this context).

It is possible to use an actual beer can and beer, but I recommend purchasing a purpose-designed utensil from a barbecue shop and replacing the beer with wine. Beer cans are designed for beer preservation rather than cooking, and I consider the taste of beer incompatible with chicken. Obviously, if you prefer chicken infused with boiled beer, you should use beer.

The asparagusic acid in asparagus will (after processing by your body) give your urine a distinctive odor, which approximately 70% of the population is genetically configured to detect. There is evidence that a small percentage of people process asparagusic acid differently and do not create the odor at all. An interesting topic for dinner discussion and experimentation.

COMMON RESOURCES: GRILLED ASPARAGUS

1/2 lemon
Parmesan cheese

RECIPE-SPECIFIC INGREDIENTS: GRILLED ASPARAGUS

1 bunch asparagus (I recommend thick-stemmed)

**COMMON RESOURCES:
BEER-CAN CHICKEN WITH ROAST VEGETABLES**

Quantities allow for leftovers to be deployed on Monday.
200 g potatoes
200 g pumpkin
200 g sweet potatoes
Wine
Garlic

RECIPE-SPECIFIC INGREDIENTS:
BEER-CAN CHICKEN WITH ROAST VEGETABLES

1.6 kg[1] raw chicken
1/2 bunch herbs — preferably tarragon

EQUIPMENT

Commercial "beer-can" barbecue cooking apparatus
    or empty beer can
Serving plate for asparagus
Serving plate for chicken and roast vegetables
Small plate
Grater
Bowl
Meat thermometer
Carving knife and fork
Lemon squeezer

PROCESS

*Time: 2 hours, including at least 35 minutes
unallocated time.*

Do not start unless you know how to carve a chicken
(google instructional video if necessary).

0: Remove chicken from refrigerator.

20 minutes unallocated time.

21: Activate barbecue — lid on, all burners on maximum.
    When 200 degrees is attained, turn off central
    burner(s). Monitor to maintain 190—205 degrees.
    If necessary, supplement side burners with central
    burners set low.

---

[1] Second reminder: approximately.

27: Half-fill beer-can reservoir with wine and insert herbs with stalks intact.

Lower chicken onto vertical beer can / equipment — can goes into cavity.

Rub chicken with 1 tablespoon of olive oil, then 1 teaspoon of salt and product of 4 twists of pepper grinder.

30: Open barbecue lid; place chicken assembly over central barbecue burners; close barbecue lid.

45: Heat oven to 220 degrees.

47: Cut lemon (if not already cut) and squeeze. Pour juice on asparagus plate and add 2 tablespoons of olive oil. If asparagus is the thick variety, break each stalk at the weakest point and discard thicker part. Put asparagus in oil and lemon juice, and turn each stalk to contact the marinade. Return unused lemon half to refrigerator for drinks or future cooking.

52: Peel potatoes and cut into 3 cm cubes. Peel sweet potatoes and pumpkin, and cut into 5 cm cubes. Chop 3 cloves of garlic into tiny pieces (1 minute); put garlic, 3 tablespoons of cooking oil, and vegetable pieces into bowl, and stir 15 seconds.

57: Put 2 tablespoons of cooking oil on oven tray and place in oven.

60: Open oven and pour contents of bowl (root vegetables) onto oven tray. Distribute with spatula to create a single layer.

76: Put asparagus on barbecue over hot burners (at 90 degrees to grill bars, to prevent falling through). Do not discard marinade.

78: Grate 2 tablespoons of parmesan cheese onto small plate.

80: Turn asparagus 180 degrees with spatula.

82: Turn root vegetables 180 degrees with spatula.

84: Remove asparagus from barbecue with spatula and return to marinade. Turn to coat with surplus lemon juice and oil. Sprinkle over the parmesan cheese. Eat with fingers. (Don't forget to take time out to check the chicken — next step.)

90: Clean fingers. Insert thermometer at thickest part of chicken thigh (not touching bone). Monitor every 10 minutes. When temperature reaches 70 degrees, turn off burners.

Minimum fifteen minutes free time.

Allow chicken to rest fifteen minutes or until temperature has risen to 74 degrees minimum (whichever is later).

Turn oven temperature to low to enable potatoes to remain warm until chicken is ready.

When chicken is ready: carve; *do not discard carcass*.

Serve half the chicken meat with half the root vegetables.

Refrigerate remainder of meat, vegetables, and chicken carcass.

VARIATIONS

Put 1/2 a tablespoon of truffle oil on the asparagus before adding the cheese.

Squeeze the spare half-lemon over the chicken after carving.

If the barbecue is sufficiently large — or you have multiple barbecues, as I do — the vegetables can be barbecued in the roasting dish.

Rub the chicken with a spice mixture, e.g. commercial "roast chicken spice mix" or chili salt (refer margarita recipe, Spring Tuesday), instead of salt and pepper.

Order the chicken "butterflied" and adjust barbecuing process to allow 23 minutes each side over medium direct barbecue heat. The chicken can be marinated for 4 hours in advance in 100 ml of lemon juice, 100 ml of olive oil, and 18 twists of the pepper grinder.

If you require a green vegetable with the main course, I recommend grilling 2 zucchinis cut lengthwise into 1 cm slices on the barbecue or adding them whole to the roast-vegetable pan during the final 20 minutes of chicken cooking.

SPRING SUNDAY:

Barbecued Flounder with Steamed Vegetables; Mango Sorbet

Preparation for Wednesday and
Common Resource Maintenance:

> Roast-chicken Stock (minimum 4 hours cooking
> required, though only 7 minutes work)

Other Common Resource Maintenance, if required:

> Frozen Mango (requires 6 hours to freeze —
> relevant if needed for tonight)

Tonight's meal is a perfect illustration of the adaptability of the Standardized Meal System. The fish can be virtually any variety of whole fish or fish fillets. In fact, it is possible to substitute other kinds of seafood, meat, vegetables, or even Greek frying cheese. If this is done, obviously the meal can no longer be referred to as Barbecued Flounder.

Flounder, world's best whitefish, has the advantage of being a flexible conversation starter. I recommend the following thirteen[1] flounder-inspired discussions.

1. Cooks are routinely advised that it is better to undercook than overcook fish. Does flounder taste better undercooked or overcooked? (Provide samples.)

2. The flounder provides evidence of evolution: one eye has migrated from the opposite side of the head to support the flatfish swimming configuration,

---

[1] Limited to one year's suggestions by the editor, who is in favor of changing fish, not just annually but weekly! I recommend you use the first discussion of the next year to brainstorm twelve further topics. This approach can also be used if you choose an alternative to flounder.

but not to the extent of being symmetrical with the other eye. A designer would presumably have made the eyes symmetrical[1].

3. Non-symmetrical eyes are widely considered unattractive. Why do humans correlate symmetry with beauty?

4. Symmetry is common in nature. Why?

5. Are flounder(s) all asymmetrical in the same way or are some (what percentage?) mirror images of each other? Does this result apply to all flatfish species? How can it be explained?

6. Is the flounder asymmetrical when it hatches or does the asymmetry develop?

7. Most fish swim in an orientation rotated 90 degrees from that of the flounder. What advantages are there in the different configurations?

8. Some people refuse to eat a fish with its head (including eyes) in place. What is the source of this revulsion? What taboos would diners break if starving?

9. Is the plural of *flounder flounder* or *flounders*? Does this ambiguity apply to other fish? Why?

10. Is the fish the origin of the verb *to flounder*? Would communication be simpler if words could not have multiple meanings?

11. The term *flounder* covers several species, some only distantly related. Should we revise the naming of fish (and biological taxonomies in general) in the light of DNA comparisons?

---

[1] I recommend Policansky, D. The Asymmetry of Flounders, *Scientific American*, 246 (5), 1982, pp. 116—23, as a reference on this matter.

12. What is flounder roe? What are the differences between male and female roe? Is your meal male or female? (Roe is even more delicious than flounder flesh and the discussion may prompt other diners to give theirs to you.)

13. How well would flounder-shaped tiles cover a floor? How could the flounder shape be modified to achieve 100% coverage?

RECIPE-SPECIFIC INGREDIENTS: STEAMED VEGETABLES

8 small new potatoes
100 g green beans

COMMON RESOURCES: FLOUNDER

4 tbsp plain flour

RECIPE-SPECIFIC INGREDIENTS: FLOUNDER

2 whole flounder(s), cleaned and scaled by fishmonger

COMMON RESOURCES: MANGO SORBET

200 g frozen mango
Sprig (3 or 4 joined leaves) of mint (optional)

EQUIPMENT

Plastic or paper bag large enough to contain one flounder
Plate
Steamer
Serving plate for vegetables
Food processor
Flounder(s) require large plates: I suggest serving the fish onto them rather than centrally

PROCESS

Time: 44 minutes, plus 5 minutes to prepare dessert.

0: Activate steamer and put in new potatoes (no need to peel first). Sprinkle with salt.

Chop ends off beans.

25: Heat barbecue plate (not the grill) to medium heat. Add 2 tablespoons of cooking oil.

27: Put half of the flour in the bag with first flounder and shake to coat the flounder in flour. Repeat for second flounder.

30: Put both flounder(s) on barbecue plate.

32: Add beans to steamer. Sprinkle with salt.

36.5: Turn flounder(s) with barbecue spatula.

41: Serve vegetables.

43: Serve flounder.

When ready for dessert: put frozen mango pieces in food processor. Process until the consistency of sorbet. Put into cocktail coupes or conventional bowls. If you have mint (e.g. growing in garden), add a sprig to each. Serve.

VARIATIONS

Butter can be used in place of oil (or mixed with oil to prevent burning) to cook the flounder. Butter can also be added to the new potatoes (optionally with parsley) when serving.

Add 15 ml (maximum 1/4 standard drink per person) liqueur to the mango slices before blending. I recommend coconut (Malibu) or orange (Cointreau, Grand Marnier). If using peaches instead of mangoes, I recommend amaretto.

COMMON RESOURCE MAINTENANCE: FROZEN MANGO (4 MINUTES WORK)

If you have exhausted your supply of frozen mango slices, schedule this task at least 6 hours in advance of tonight's dinner to allow freezing time. Otherwise, it can be done at any time.

The total requirement for the season is 13 serves of 200 g flesh (approximately the yield from a medium mango), 2.6 kg in total. I recommend preparing a single serve the first week to enable refining (or deletion) of the amount after eating for the first time. After that, you can prepare any proportion of the remaining requirement.

RECIPE–SPECIFIC INGREDIENTS

Ripe mangoes (see above for quantity)

EQUIPMENT

Freezer containers / bags

PROCESS

Cut mango flesh from stone (4 pieces per mango, once you're familiar with the size of a mango stone, but smaller pieces are equally good). Use knife to remove flesh from skin. Freeze flesh in batches of 200 g. Discard skin and stone.

VARIATION

Use peaches (peeled and stoned) instead of mangoes. Other stone fruit may also work.

PREPARATION FOR WEDNESDAY AND COMMON RESOURCE MAINTENANCE: ROAST-CHICKEN STOCK

This recipe utilizes the chicken carcass from Saturday. You can optionally include leftovers (bones) from diners' plates — my grandmother did this, but my mother considered it unhygienic. I follow my grandmother's practice in a household which already shares pathogens.

The quantity from one chicken carcass is sufficient for two meals. It is useful to build a stockpile, as it is required all year, but you can discard the carcass if you have enough already frozen. Conversely, if you don't make stock at least every second week, you will run out. In that case, take one of the following actions (in descending order of acceptability):

1. Use the large-quantity chicken-stock recipe specified on Summer Sunday.
2. Purchase commercial chicken stock.
3. Use stock cube / powder, following instructions on packaging.
4. Use water (surprisingly successful in most dishes).

COMMON RESOURCES

2 brown onions
2 carrots

RECIPE-SPECIFIC INGREDIENTS

Leftover chicken carcass

EQUIPMENT

Pot large enough to easily contain chicken carcass
(squashed) with lid
Bowl
Sieve
Freezer container, 500 ml

PROCESS

*Time: minimum 4 3/4 hours, plus 5 minutes before bed.
Less than 15 minutes actual work.*

Peel and cut onions into 8 pieces each. Cut carrots
into 1 cm discs.

Put onion and chicken carcass in pot. Squash down
chicken with hand (1 or 2 presses are sufficient —
break the carcass into pieces if it fails to compress).

Add cold water to 5 cm above maximum height
of chicken — about 8 cups.

Put lid on pot and set temperature to simmer. Normally,
in making stock, you need to skim the scum which rises
to the surface, but with the pre-cooking of the chicken
there will be minimal scum to skim. Leave to simmer for
at least 4 hours.

Turn off heat. Allow to cool for 30 minutes. Set timer!

Pour liquid through sieve into bowl, cover with cling
wrap, and refrigerate. Discard contents of sieve and
any onion or chicken remaining in pot. Set timer for
just prior to bedtime.

When timer sounds: with a spoon, remove fat from
surface and discard. Measure 500 ml and keep in
refrigerator for soup on Wednesday. Freeze remainder.

Chicken and Roast-vegetable Salad

Monday evenings are disproportionately susceptible to being disrupted by problems, often due to the working / school week beginning with some announcement. Accordingly, I schedule simple meals which can be prepared and eaten quickly.

Tonight's is an example — delicious but simple, leveraging the effort of the weekend. It can readily be varied. My mother would add canned beetroot (a good product, though inferior to beetroot purchased fresh or pre-cooked) and I also do so, but almost any fresh vegetable will work. If it requires cooking, cook it.

COMMON RESOURCES

1 tbsp pepitas
1 tbsp sunflower seeds
1 tsp chia seeds
120 g feta cheese (preferably marinated)
1 tbsp red-wine vinegar

RECIPE-SPECIFIC INGREDIENTS

Leftover roast vegetables and chicken
100 g baby-spinach leaves

EQUIPMENT

Salad bowl
Salad servers

PROCESS

Time: 4 minutes.

Put roast vegetables, spinach leaves, and any optional vegetables into salad bowl. Add 1 tablespoon of red-wine vinegar and "toss" (mix) with salad servers. Add 2 tablespoons of olive oil (or feta–cheese marinade) and toss again. Add chicken and toss a third time. Sprinkle feta and seeds on top.

VARIATIONS

Use a flavored oil such as basil oil, or add fresh basil leaves.

Use alternative flavored vinegar.

Chorizo Dates; Chermoula-spiced Salmon with Couscous; Turkish Delight

Guest night. Quantity for four people.

Recommended cocktail: pomegranate margarita.

Recommended wine: pinot noir.

My mother always cooked the most complicated meals — often using unfamiliar recipes — when we had guests, in violation of her stated belief that "family comes first." As a result, she was frequently agitated and absent from the table.

The Standardized Meal System eliminates this problem. The lack-of-familiarity issue diminishes with weekly repetition (for regular guests also). This meal is designed so that most of the work can be performed before guests arrive. The salmon will cook without intervention while the dates are being eaten. Criticism is reduced to virtually zero by the margaritas.

The margarita is among the world's most popular cocktails and guests frequently observe that my margaritas are superior to any they have previously tasted. The reason is usually that they are accustomed to the versions served in generic Mexican (or Tex-Mex) restaurants, which typically consist of a shot of tequila heavily diluted with fruit squash or sweet-and-sour mix. For the same reason, they are often surprised by the impact of the alcohol in an authentic margarita.

As with almost all cocktails[1], the most critical ingredient

---

[1] Most cocktails are served chilled. Notable exceptions include those in the pousse-café (layered) category, not currently fashionable.

is the cheapest: ice. Too high a temperature will negate the value of expensive liquor. If the glass is rimmed with salt, the effect will be akin to drinking warm seawater, a traditional emetic[1].

Some margarita connoisseurs object to salting the glass. I recommend salting half the rim, giving drinkers a choice. With the pomegranate margarita (in fact, all margaritas), I use chili salt[2].

Quantities are for 1 standard drink. If you are not adding pomegranate juice, this will only partially fill a typical margarita glass, so I suggest either allowing 2 standard drinks per person or diluting (see below).

DON TILLMAN'S MARGARITA INGREDIENTS (ONE STANDARD DRINK)

12 ml freshly squeezed lime juice[3]
    (retain 2 lime halves after squeezing)
9 ml Cointreau (variation: 6 ml Cointreau,
    3 ml Blood Orange Cointreau)
15 ml silver tequila
6 ml mezcal
For the pomegranate variant, 30 ml commercial
    unsweetened pomegranate juice

---

[1] Use of saltwater to induce vomiting is (like many traditional remedies) dangerous and potentially fatal, not only because of the risk of salt poisoning, but also because it takes the place of more effective medical treatment.

[2] Pound 2 parts of flaky salt with 1 part of dried whole chilies or chili flakes in a mortar and pestle until it looks fine enough to stick to a glass. Alternatively, purchase commercial chili salt.

[3] There is an argument that the lime juice should be aged for several hours to permit enzymatic bittering. I consider fresh juice superior, but the Standardized Meal System provides a basis for experimentation.

These ingredients can be mixed in advance of guests arriving and stored in the refrigerator. The glasses can also be prepared beforehand:

Spread salt (1/2 a teaspoon per glass) on chopping board over an area of 3 x 1 cm. Wet rims of glasses with the post–squeezing lime halves (or water). Dip half (180 degrees) of each rim in the salt. Put glasses in freezer.

When ready to serve, quarter–fill the cocktail shaker with ice and add ingredients (excluding salt). Shake for at least 45 seconds. Pour into glasses.

Diluting a margarita:

In my experience, it is possible to add unobtrusive lime squash to a standard margarita without detection (except in a contemporaneous comparison with the undiluted version) if the quantity does not exceed 25% of the original volume. Inexperienced margarita drinkers or those accustomed to restaurant margaritas will not notice even greater dilutions.

I suggest experimenting with replacing some of the tequila with mezcal (up to 100%), as the smokier taste of the mezcal will better survive dilution.

I recommend the following recipe for lime squash:

100 ml lime juice; 50 ml agave nectar, dissolved in 150 ml hot water; 200 ml additional water; mix and chill.

Another possibility is to add fruit juice in the same proportions as the pomegranate juice to create (for example) a guava, grapefruit, or mango margarita.

RECIPE–SPECIFIC INGREDIENTS: CHORIZO DATES

12 dates
1 chorizo sausage (smoked, not requiring cooking)

COMMON RESOURCES: CHERMOULA SALMON

Chermoula paste
Harissa paste (put on table with spoon)

RECIPE–SPECIFIC INGREDIENTS: CHERMOULA SALMON

900 g salmon fillet, including skin (allows for leftovers)

COMMON RESOURCES: COUSCOUS

300 g couscous
1 lemon
100 g pitted green olives
50 g dried cranberries or cherries
80 g pistachio nuts (shelled)

RECIPE–SPECIFIC INGREDIENTS: COUSCOUS

1/2 bunch coriander leaves
1/2 bunch mint
1 red capsicum
4 spring onions

COMMON RESOURCES: TURKISH DELIGHT

12 pieces commercial Turkish delight

EQUIPMENT

Small sharp knife
Kettle
Medium saucepan

Bowl

Cooking foil

Small plate for serving dates

Platter for serving salmon and couscous

Small plate for serving Turkish delight

PROCESS

*Time: 12 minutes pre-guest-arrival preparation,
plus 37 minutes.*

Prior to arrival of guests (if possible):

Prepare couscous according to the simplest recipe
on the packaging[1].

Chop olives into quarters.

Tear coriander and mint leaves from stalks.

Cut capsicum into 1/2 cm cubes[2].

Chop non-leafy part of spring onions into 1/2 cm discs.
Discard leafy (tough) part.

Put chopped ingredients in bowl with pistachios.

Slit each date with a knife to access its seed without
breaking date into pieces. Remove and discard seed.

Cut 12 date-seed-sized pieces of chorizo and insert
one in each date to replace the seed. It is normal for
some chorizo to be exposed, but the pieces should
not be at risk of falling out.

---

[1] If no recipe due to buying in bulk or discarding package to enable
safe storage: pour 2 1/4 cups of boiling water on 1 1/2 cups of
couscous, allow to stand 6 minutes, add 1 tablespoon of olive oil,
stir with fork to break up clumps and "fluff."

[2] Third reminder: approximately.

When guests arrive:

0: Activate all barbecue burners (high setting).

Prepare and serve pomegranate margaritas.

Place salmon, skin down, on a piece of foil 5 cm larger than the fillet on all sides.

10: Turn off central barbecue burners and place salmon (on foil) over the extinguished burners.

Also put dates over the (still hot) extinguished burners. (If there is a risk of them falling through the grill, put them on foil close to the direct heat.)

12: Use spatula to turn each date 180 degrees to expose uncooked side to heat.

14: Use spatula to transfer dates to the serving plate.

Serve and eat dates.

35: Tip contents of bowl into couscous and mix with fork. Tip onto salmon–serving plate and spread evenly. Squeeze the lemon over the mixture.

Turn off barbecue. Turn over salmon with spatula (the foil will stick to the salmon) to sear chermoula–covered surface for 30 seconds.

Remove salmon from barbecue with spatula onto chopping board, foil side down. (If the foil comes off with the skin, discard.) Slice off 33% of the salmon, cover with cling wrap, and refrigerate.

Cut slices of remaining salmon 1 cm thick but press only hard enough to cut through the flesh and not the skin (unless the skin has already been discarded). The flesh will detach from the skin easily. Place the slices on top of the couscous salad.

Serve and eat.

Serve Turkish delight.

Return any uneaten Turkish delight to storage.

VARIATIONS

Replace salmon with chicken fillet(s). Ensure cooked before serving (cut a cross-section if necessary).

Delete dates and fry the chorizo in slices.

Delete chorizo and serve the dates (uncooked) after the main course, with or instead of Turkish delight.

SPRING WEDNESDAY:

Mushroom Risotto with Green Salad; Chocolates

At least 91%[1] of Italians will tell you that risotto made by some individual known to them is not only superior to restaurant risotto but to all other homemade risotto. Obviously, the best way to make risotto is to learn from such an individual (e.g. my friend Sonia's aunt). It will provide interesting social interaction, possibly with an older person needing company and purpose.

They will almost certainly share interesting stories, which can be repeated when you serve the risotto (I recommend one story per occasion). And your approach to risotto making will be immune from criticism (except, of course, by Italians).

If you experience difficulty finding an expert[2], you can temporarily use a recipe from the internet or the packaging of a pre-mixed risotto product. It will provide something for your expert, when found, to criticize.

All ingredients and equipment listed below may be overridden by the risotto expert.

Chocolates are scheduled for one day per week when I consider the psychological comfort most likely to be required. You may want to vary the timing to align with stressful days in your schedule. I recommend limiting

[1] Based on my conversations with people not only born in Italy but with Italian lineage: $p=0.05$.

[2] This could be a result of living in a location with zero or close-to-zero Italians. But if you reside in a city with Italians and don't know any, I recommend broadening your social circle, using the risotto project as an excuse.

the quantity to 2 per person, and *purchasing and monitoring accordingly.*

COMMON RESOURCES

200 g arborio rice
Dried porcini mushrooms
Butter
White wine
Parmesan cheese
1 tbsp red-wine vinegar

RECIPE-SPECIFIC INGREDIENTS

500 ml homemade roast-chicken stock
Fresh ingredients specified by risotto expert
80 g rocket leaves

EQUIPMENT

Saucepan
Empty jar with lid
Salad bowl
Salad servers
Serving plate for risotto (I use the saucepan
     to avoid losing heat in transfer)

PROCESS

Time: risotto — as advised by expert. Typically 30 minutes. Add 3 minutes for salad (I do not recommend time-sharing any task with risotto making).

Vigorously shake 3 tablespoons of olive oil, the vinegar, and 1/4 teaspoon of salt in the jar (lid on) for 15 seconds. Put the leaves in the salad bowl.

Prepare the risotto (refer above).

Pour contents of jar over leaves. Toss using salad servers.

Serve risotto and salad.

Chocolates.

VARIATIONS

I have specified mushrooms as the major flavoring, but risotto is amenable to numerous variations, some of which will doubtless be suggested by the expert.

Tacos with Salmon and Guacamole

I am *stunned* at how frequently my friends and colleagues serve unmodified leftovers the following day. These are the same people who criticize the Standardized Meal System (and, by association, me) for being boring.

Both Monday's and tonight's meals utilize leftovers, but their form is significantly changed and the time lapse[1] reduces the impression of repetition. This is one of the advantages of planning. When I was a junior researcher, I made extra risotto and vinaigrette on Wednesdays, and recycled it as arancini with salad. If you want to reduce costs, or prefer arancini to salmon tacos, you should do the same.

The guacamole component should not be made in advance, as it is likely to be discovered and eaten. This will unbalance the main meal and encourage margarita consumption, which is technically not permitted on a Thursday.

COMMON RESOURCES

6 taco shells (adjust number based on experience)
1 jalapeño or alternative preferred chili, fresh, preserved, or reconstituted (optional)
1 lime (preferably) or lemon

---

[1] The (US) FDA advises that cooked seafood can safely be kept for "three to four days" in the refrigerator. Given the ambiguity in this statement and the possible consequences of misinterpretation, I recommend no more than three.

RECIPE-SPECIFIC INGREDIENTS

Leftover salmon
1 avocado (large)
Leftover spring onions (maximum 4)
Leftover coriander leaves (up to 1/2 bunch)
50 g lettuce leaves
1 medium tomato

EQUIPMENT

Bowl
Measuring spoons
Serving plate(s) for salmon, tacos, and chili
Lemon squeezer

PROCESS

Time: 30 minutes.

If using fresh chilies, chop into tiny pieces
(30 seconds chopping).

Make guacamole:

Cut avocado in half lengthwise (not through stone);
twist halves apart; pull out stone[1] and discard. Scoop
out flesh with tablespoon and put in bowl. Cut lime
in half and squeeze over avocado. Mash with fork.

Slice spring onions in small slices, as for couscous
salad, and add to bowl.

---

[1] An interesting but unreliable technique for removing the stone is
to strike it with the sharp edge of the knife, then lift the knife while
holding the avocado half. It does not always work, as the interference
fit between knife and stone may not be as strong as the fit between
avocado flesh and stone. Hence, do not perform it to demonstrate
competence.

Slice tomato into halves; squeeze out seeds
and liquid, and discard (peeling[1] is optional).
Chop into 1 cm cubes and add to bowl.

Tear coriander leaves from stalks and chop into
1/2 cm squares[2]. Add to bowl. Mix contents of
bowl with fork.

Heat taco shells in oven according to instructions.

Put tacos, lettuce leaves, and salmon on a serving
plate with guacamole and chopped chili to be
assembled by diners (they may use leaves rather
than tacos as casing).

VARIATIONS

Add cumin or coriander spices, or guacamole
spice mix, to the guacamole.

As an alternative to tacos, salmon can be
mixed with an egg and formed into fishcakes
(mashed potato can be added as required to
increase quantity). Dip in breadcrumbs (or flour
if breadcrumbs unavailable) and fry. Use lettuce
leaves to make salad.

---

[1] To peel, drop tomato into boiling water for 10 seconds
to split and loosen skin, then peel with knife or fingers.

[2] Reminder: *approximately*.

Restaurant Night or Pizza (Frozen or Delivered)

Recommended wine: red wine is mandatory, unless you don't like red wine or are avoiding alcohol. The quality can be inversely proportional to the quantity of chili on the pizza (one of the many benefits of chili is in reducing the cost of wine).

At one time I feared restaurants as minefields for the socially inept (specifically, me). No longer! Thanks to a relatively small amount of research and practice, undertaken as part of the Rosie Project, I now consider a familiar restaurant to be the perfect social setting. The protocols are straightforward and easily memorized, and I am likely to be even more comfortable with them than my companions are. In the rare event of an error, the staff will support a regular customer. I have a sense of social ease that I would not have in a less structured environment.

Commercial frozen pizza or home-delivered pizza is generally of lower quality than the version eaten fresh at your favorite pizza restaurant. The choice of inferior products is deliberate. You should be motivated but not forced to eat out. Friday meals are backups to the preferred option of seeking tastier, healthier, and potentially more social alternatives — and exercising the related social skills.

If you choose the delivery option, and the pizza is taking a long time to arrive, you may serve some of the antipasto items as a starter to accompany the wine.

COMMON RESOURCES

Frozen pizza only: antipasto items (salumi, preserved
vegetables) from refrigerator and jars

Frozen or delivered pizza: some form of chili
(Preferably fresh, chopped, but flakes or
reconstituted dried chilies or chili–infused
oil are acceptable. Marinated chilies, including
the oil, are excellent. I do not recommend
chili paste for this purpose.)

EQUIPMENT

Serving plate or board for pizza
(to facilitate slicing)

Specialized pizza–slicing roller
(optional — knife is adequate)

PROCESS

*Time: typically 10 minutes for frozen pizza;
indefinite time for delivered version.*

Select one option:

1. Phone pizza vendor and heat oven to
    160 degrees. When pizza arrives, check
    temperature and reheat in oven if required.

2. Remove frozen pizza from freezer and add
    antipasto ingredients to make it more interesting.
    Cook according to instructions on package.

Add preferred amount of chili. Eat pizza.
Drink wine. Discuss psychological reasons for
not eating out and develop plan for resolving.

SUMMER

SATURDAY
Lunch
Poke bowl

Dinner
Greek-style barbecue

SUNDAY
Thai duck / chicken curry
Grilled pineapple

MONDAY
Greek gazpacho
Barbecued-vegetable ratatouille

TUESDAY
(guests)
Grilled figs
Lobster salad
Cheese and crackers
Piña-colada sorbet

WEDNESDAY
Barbecued pork with watermelon salad
Chocolates

THURSDAY
Parmesan crisps and prosciutto
Spaghetti puttanesca with green salad

FRIDAY
(if eating at home)
Minestrone

SUMMER SATURDAY LUNCH:

Poke Bowl

This recipe contains "sashimi-grade" tuna, which can be replaced with salmon (also "sashimi-grade") if tuna is unavailable or you prefer salmon. I was once severely criticized for ordering bluefin tuna at a restaurant[1], as the fish is critically endangered (though the fate of the individual fish in question had already been determined). Fortunately, having since tasted bluefin tuna[2], I prefer the yellowfin (ahi) variety, which is less fatty and not endangered. Rosie formerly ate only sustainable seafood and no meat, for ethical reasons. Yet living an ethical life, taking into account harm to animals and risks of extinction, is incredibly difficult.

Are we only trying to avoid complete extinction, or is there merit in encouraging more of a species to be born? Including humans, given that many of the sustainability problems would disappear if the human population diminished? Are the lives of all animals and fish — and even insects and plankters — of equal value? If not, how do we calculate individual worth and the appropriate (relative) level of empathy and concern? Is intelligence a relevant input? Ability to feel pain? Cuteness? Should we kill predators to save the lives of their prey? Must our decisions be scalable? Or can we personally take non-scalable decisions, such as eating kangaroo, which does not consume the farmed grain that generates mouse plagues,

---

[1] The Bluefin Tuna Incident is documented in *The Rosie Effect*.

[2] Also documented in *The Rosie Effect*. The fish was purchased by Rosie, who gave greater weight to enhancing our relationship than to her contribution to the extinction of a species.

leading to the deliberate mass poisoning and agonizing deaths of millions of animals which would otherwise never have been born, and which I know from personal experience to be relatively intelligent and even "cute," almost certainly more so than bluefin tuna?

Rosie and I have discussed these and a vast number of related issues, such as whether our decision to have only one child and cycle to work entitles us to wreak some compensatory damage in the interests of a tastier meal, at length. The net result is that Rosie now eats a limited amount of meat and the topic is no longer permitted to be raised.

Note the use of the rice cooker. *All* of my Asian friends — and their *mothers*, who would be expected to be reference points for tradition — use this inexpensive appliance. Several recommend scheduling at least 15 minutes in "warm" mode before serving the rice.

COMMON RESOURCES

2/3 cup brown rice
2 tbsp soy sauce
1 tbsp sesame oil
1 lime

RECIPE-SPECIFIC INGREDIENTS

200 g (1 or 2 slices) yellowfin tuna (or alternative, according to taste and ethics)
1 birds-eye or alternative preferred chili, fresh or reconstituted (optional)
1 avocado
1 cob of sweet corn
1 red capsicum (only 1/2 required today)

EQUIPMENT

Rice cooker with plastic ladle
Medium bowl

PROCESS

Time: 35 minutes, largely determined by rice-cooking time, with some unallocated time.

Put brown rice in the rice cooker with a cup of water (more than required for white rice; it will cause the cooking time to lengthen, as the cooker's cutoff is triggered by temperature rather than time) and activate[1].

Chop chili into tiny pieces (30 seconds) and put in bowl.

Add sesame oil and soy sauce to bowl; mix with spoon.

Cut the tuna into 1 cm cubes and add to the bowl. Stir to cover tuna in dressing.

Halve avocado; remove flesh using a tablespoon and cut into 1 cm cubes.

Strip leaves from sweet corn, hold on its end on a chopping board, and use knife to "shave off" the kernels. Retrieve stray kernels from bench and floor, and put in bin or with other kernels, depending on your attitude to hygiene and waste.

Chop half the capsicum into pieces the size of corn kernels. Wrap other half in cling wrap and refrigerate.

When rice is ready, distribute into 2 bowls. Add remaining ingredients, including dressing and juice of lime, on top of rice. Serve.

---

[1] If the result is unsatisfactory (due to variations in rice and rice cookers), try soaking the rice for 30 minutes, then using only 2/3 cup of water for the cooking process. Or chilling the water first. Or use white rice.

VARIATIONS

This recipe accommodates enormous variation through adding / deleting compatible ingredients, such as halved cherry tomatoes, seaweed, even nuts or pumpkin seeds. Check the internet or the menu board at a poke restaurant.

Use sushi rice and follow preparation instructions on package, including use of sushi vinegar.

SUMMER SATURDAY DINNER:

Greek-style Barbecue

One of the most common criticisms of the Standardized Meal System is its supposed lack of flexibility — a criticism comprehensively demolished by the Greek-style barbecue. This meal will improve your tolerance for ambiguity and provide enjoyable social interaction.

The source of the flexibility and social interaction is the shopping procedure, optionally preceded by negotiation with other diners. For example:

Me: Meat, seafood, or vegetables?

Rosie: Ah, it's Greek-barbecue night.

Me: Of course. It's summer. It's Saturday.

Rosie: You know the answer. Just not meat.

Me: So, complete flexibility as long as it's not meat?

Rosie: I'm guessing that'll mean calamari. And saganaki.

Me: They satisfy the criteria, so obviously I'll include them in the options.

...

Seafood Vendor: Greetings, Don. Greek-barbecue night coming up?

Me: Correct. What do you recommend?

Seafood Vendor: You asking me? I already cleaned and wrapped the calamari for you. But, doesn't matter. I've got some beautiful fresh —

Me (exhibiting *empathy*): Obviously, if you've already prepared the calamari...

Other (theoretical) possibilities include fish (whole or filleted), prawns (shrimp), mussels, scallops, lamb chops; as well as less traditional options, such as kangaroo, sausages (skinless or skinned), steak, butterflied quail, capsicums, eggplant, corn. (People of Greek heritage eat a wide variety of foods.)

Seek the vendor's advice on cooking new ingredients, as I did eighteen years ago, when I first purchased calamari.

The (optional) starter is sourced from a Greek delicatessen. The varied items available will further multiply the possibilities of this already flexible meal. Example:

Greek Deli Owner: Don. How's Rosie; how's your boy?

<Conversation unrelated to the Standardized Meal System>

Greek Deli Owner: I better serve these other customers. I've got your cheese. Three slices.

Me: What else do you recommend?

Greek Deli Owner: The dips, the marinated octopus, stuffed peppers. And here, try this dolmade. My grandmother...

<Break in conversation while dolmade is assessed>

Me: Delicious. But inferior to the frying cheese. World's most delicious Greek deli item.

Greek Deli Owner: You can't go past the cheese.

COMMON RESOURCES: GREEK BARBECUE

2 lemons
Plain flour (if Greek deli items
    include frying cheese)

RECIPE-SPECIFIC INGREDIENTS: GREEK BARBECUE

Greek deli items (e.g. frying cheese)
Greek barbecue item(s)

COMMON RESOURCES: GREEK SALAD

1 tsp oregano (dried is acceptable)
1 tbsp red-wine vinegar
150 g feta cheese (marinated or unmarinated)
28 pitted black olives (marinated or unmarinated)

RECIPE-SPECIFIC INGREDIENTS: GREEK SALAD

(Deliberately excessive to allow for leftovers)
450 g high-quality tomatoes
350 g cucumber
6 large basil leaves (or equivalent
    in small leaves)

EQUIPMENT

Salad bowl
Salad servers
Serving plate for Greek deli items
Serving plate for barbecued food
Grater / zester
Bowl for refrigerating "leftover" salad

PROCESS: GREEK SALAD

Time: 7 minutes.

Slice cucumber (peeling not required) into
1 1/2 cm cubes.

Cut tomatoes into convenient sizes for eating.
If using cherry tomatoes, cut in half.

Tear basil leaves to produce 24 pieces.

Cut feta into 1 1/2 cm cubes (if not already cut).

Put cucumber, tomatoes, olives, and basil into
bowl. Add vinegar, olive oil, and 1 teaspoon
of salt, and mix for 15 seconds with salad servers.

Transfer 300 g of salad to bowl; cover and
refrigerate for use on Monday.

Add the feta and distribute oregano over
the top.

PROCESS: GREEK BARBECUE

*Time: dependent on choice of barbecue items, but
between 10 and 40 minutes, unless cooking multiple
items serially.*

If you are cooking meat (including chicken) or prawns,
I recommend marinating it after bringing it home —
in 4 tablespoons of olive oil, 1 teaspoon of oregano
or finely chopped rosemary (meat only), 6 twists of
the pepper mill, 2 cloves of finely chopped garlic,
and the zest of the lemons. Refrigerate until an hour
before cooking.

Slice lemons into quarters and put on serving plate
for barbecued food.

If you are having a starter:

>If you have selected frying cheese:

>>Put 2 tablespoons of flour on chopping board, wet cheese under the tap, then place each side in contact with the flour to coat.

>>Fry cheese on barbecue plate (or in frying pan) on high heat for 3 minutes each side, using spatula to flip.

>>Serve and squeeze a wedge of lemon over cheese.

>Else:

>>Put Greek deli items on serving plate.

>Commence eating while working at barbecue.

Cook the Greek barbecue item(s) as recommended by the vendor and serve. Eat with salad. Diners should squeeze lemon juice on all items.

If there are diverse items (e.g. lamb chops and fish), I recommend cooking each variety separately and eating it before cooking the next, assuming diners are eating in the vicinity of the barbecue and can continue conversation with you. If not (e.g. unsuitable weather; poor house design or selection), I recommend calculating start times for all items so that they finish together.

None of this complexity is necessary if you have standardized on calamari.

If there is leftover salad (even just liquid), remove the feta cheese (discard / eat) and add to the bowl in the refrigerator.

VARIATION

This meal already accommodates vast variation.

SUMMER SUNDAY:

Thai Duck / Chicken Curry; Grilled Pineapple

Common Resource Maintenance, if required — *start early!*

Chicken Stock

Minestrone Soup

Thai and *curry* are both strongly correlated with *chili*. My position on chili is similar to my friend Dave's position on bacon: as an additive, it has the potential to improve most savory dishes. When forced to eat mass-produced food that has been designed to be inoffensive to the maximum number of people (hence *zero* spice, *zero* interesting ingredients, and overcooked), I pack a vial of cayenne pepper to add to my meal (more practical than bacon). If you do not want to stimulate a discussion, or criticism, I recommend performing this act surreptitiously (virtually impossible with bacon).

The instructions are for the duck version. If using chicken, check under Variations — changes are minor.

COMMON RESOURCES: THAI DUCK / CHICKEN CURRY

3/4 cup rice of your preferred variety[1]
Thai yellow-curry paste
1 tbsp fish sauce
2 limes
1 cup coconut milk — store remainder
of 400 ml can in refrigerator
3 frozen kaffir-lime leaves (can be
omitted if impossible to source)

---

[1] I use basmati rice. But you are free to use any or multiple varieties, and to configure the rice cooker accordingly.

RECIPE-SPECIFIC INGREDIENTS:
THAI DUCK / CHICKEN CURRY

300 g duck fillet (boneless breast, skin on)
1/2 red capsicum (leftover)
2 red and / or yellow capsicums
200 g snake beans or conventional green beans
1 bunch coriander leaves

RECIPE-SPECIFIC INGREDIENTS: GRILLED PINEAPPLE

1 ripe pineapple

EQUIPMENT

Rice cooker with plastic ladle
Large frying pan or wok
Small sharp knife
Plate
Small bowl
Blender or food processor
Freezer container or bag (approx. 300 ml)

PROCESS

Time: 63 minutes, including at least 30 minutes unallocated time.

At any time: chop both ends off pineapple and slice down sides to remove all skin. Slice two 2 cm discs from the pineapple, remove tough cores with a sharp knife, cover with cling wrap, and refrigerate. Slice remainder of pineapple into 2 1/2 cm discs, cut around core to remove edible flesh, and chop that into cubes[1] (approximately 200 g). Freeze the cubes for Tuesday.

---

[1] Periodic reminder: *approximate* cubes.

0: Set oven to 175 degrees.

Put rice in cooker with equal volume of water and activate.

Trim ends from beans. Optionally, cut into thirds (but whole snake beans look more interesting).

Cut capsicums in half (except the one already halved), remove seeds and pith, and cut into 1 cm cubes.

Tear coriander leaves from stalks.

Cut lime into quarters and put on table.

Slash duck skin with knife — 4 parallel cuts, 4 more at 90 degrees — to enable fat to escape when cooking.

12: Put duck on oven tray (or in a roasting dish), fat side down.

Free time.

42: Put frying pan on burner / hotplate with heat at 40% of maximum.

Remove duck from oven. Transfer 2 tablespoons of duck fat from oven tray to frying pan.

45: Put 4 tablespoons of curry paste in the pan. Stir with wooden spoon.

47: Add coconut milk, fish sauce, lime leaves torn in half, beans, capsicum, and 150 ml of water. Stir.

Cut duck fillet in half crosswise, then into 1 cm slices along (previously) long dimension. Add duck to pan and stir.

Adjust temperature to maintain simmer.

62: Put rice on table.

Sprinkle coriander leaves over curry and serve. Advise diners to squeeze lime on their portions.

When guests are ready for dessert: heat barbecue grill to medium, put pineapple slices on, cook for 2 minutes each side, and serve.

VARIATIONS

Replace duck with chicken. You will not need to slash the skin to release fat, but in the absence of duck fat will need to use cooking oil or coconut oil sourced by separating coconut cream, which could be sourced from fresh coconut. If you are contemplating the latter option, you should consult a specialist Thai cookery book.

Add birds−eye chili or reconstituted dried chili at the same time as the beans (recommended).

Experiment with alternative brands of curry paste, and with red and green varieties.

Add a stalk of lemongrass cut into 5 cm lengths.

A variety of other vegetables can be added. I recommend baby corn, eggplant, and sweet potato (pre−boil in small pieces).

Roast a banana on the barbecue in its skin for 20 minutes and add to the curry just before serving.

Pineapple can be served raw rather than grilled. Or, after turning the pineapple over, pour 1/2 a tablespoon of dark rum on each slice (there will be flames).

COMMON RESOURCE MAINTENANCE: MINESTRONE SOUP

This recipe makes approximately 32 cups (16 serves) of soup, which can be frozen — enough for eight Friday meals for two. The quantity will fit in a 30 cm diameter x 12 1/2 cm high pot; if you are using a smaller pot, scale down.

However, minestrone is the world's most relaxing (and potentially therapeutic and creativity–enhancing[1]) dish to prepare — routine work which does not require precision in timing or quantity[2]. You may wish to make it more frequently in smaller quantities and / or use the surplus for weekday lunches, as I do.

COMMON RESOURCES

300 g brown onions
3 carrots
3 cans tomatoes, 400g each
3 cans white beans[3], 400g each
600 g green cabbage
500 g potatoes
6 cups chicken stock (see Common
    Resource Maintenance, below)

RECIPE–SPECIFIC INGREDIENTS

600 g zucchinis
300 g green beans

---

[1] There is substantial research to indicate that creativity is facilitated by routine physical work, e.g. driving, walking, cooking.

[2] If, conversely, you find precision relaxing, you can measure quantities and time precisely.

[3] Alternatively, soak approximately 300 g dried white beans overnight, the night before. Add to task list.

EQUIPMENT

Large enameled cast-iron pot
Freezer containers (to hold 2 serves of soup — 4 cups)

PROCESS

Time: minimum 6 hours, preferably longer, but you need to be present only for the first 40 minutes, and to terminate the cooking process and freeze soup.

Put 2 tablespoons of cooking oil in pot on burner / hotplate at 60% of maximum temperature. In sequence, prepare each of the vegetables as specified below, add to pot, and stir with wooden spoon. Timing is non-critical.

Onions — peel and cut into 1 cm cubes.

Carrots — peel and cut into discs 1/2 cm thick.

Zucchini — cut into discs 1/2 cm thick.

Green beans — cut off stringy ends and halve.

Potatoes — peel and cut into 2 cm cubes.

Cabbage — cut into 1 cm slices, which will then partially disintegrate (and compress).

Continue to cook for 15 minutes, stirring every 3 minutes.

Drain liquid from white beans and add to pot.
Add tomatoes and stock.

Manage temperature to achieve and maintain simmer.

Leave to cook as long as practicable (I recommend turning it off 40 minutes before going to bed).

Turn off heat. Set timer for 5 minutes before bedtime. When timer sounds, freeze or refrigerate (see above).

COMMON RESOURCE MAINTENANCE: CHICKEN STOCK

In summer, autumn, and winter, since I do not have roast-chicken leftovers, I make stock using raw chicken. The negative is that the stock needs to be skimmed; the positive is that the recipe is totally scalable — the quantity is limited only by the capacity of your cooking pot(s) and freezer. Obviously, the frequency of replenishment will be inversely proportional to the batch quantity.

The stock will keep for 6 months in a refrigerator freezer. Do not store it in the refrigerator for more than 3 days without reheating — it is an excellent environment for breeding bacteria. Refer Spring Sunday for substitutes.

COMMON RESOURCES

4 brown onions
4 carrots

RECIPE-SPECIFIC INGREDIENTS

8 chicken carcasses (alternatively, 4 kg chicken wings)

EQUIPMENT

Largest available pot
Second-largest pot or largest bowl (whichever is larger), multiple if necessary, to hold strained stock
Large sieve
Freezer containers (to hold 2 cups each)

PROCESS

Time: minimum 5 hours, requiring occasional presence for scum skimming, plus later intervention to skim fat and freeze.

Put chicken carcasses in pot and press down to crush using hand or wooden spoon.

Peel onions and carrots.

Chop onions into quarters (or smaller) and carrots into 1 cm discs. Add to pot.

Pour cold water into pot to a level 5 cm above the top of the chicken carcasses.

Put pot on burner / hotplate on medium heat. Allow to boil; adjust heat to maintain simmer[1].

Every 15 minutes for first hour, skim denatured protein (scum) from surface with small sieve. After first hour, reduce frequency to once every 30 minutes.

After minimum 4 hours: remove pot from heat and allow to cool.

An hour later: pour liquid through sieve into second pot or bowl. Refrigerate. Set timer for just before bedtime.

When timer sounds, skim fat from surface and discard. Distribute stock into freezing containers and freeze.

---

[1] More vigorous boiling will cause the denatured protein to be incorporated into the stock, which is not harmful but renders it cloudy and aesthetically less appealing. It also wastes energy.

SUMMER MONDAY:

Greek Gazpacho;
Barbecued–vegetable Ratatouille

Tonight's meal is readily scaled up. I recommend that if you need to feed vegetarians, you schedule them for this day, move the piña–colada sorbet to today, and enjoy Tuesday's lobster undisturbed.

Greek gazpacho is an idea from chef Jamie Oliver — brilliant use of leftovers and trivially simple to make.

Ratatouille is conventionally cooked in a pan with olive oil, but in summer I take advantage of opportunities to use the barbecue, thus establishing a second "happy place" for myself.

RECIPE–SPECIFIC INGREDIENTS: GREEK GAZPACHO

Leftover ("reserved") salad from Saturday

COMMON RESOURCES: RATATOUILLE

1 large red onion
3 cloves garlic
1 tbsp balsamic vinegar
1 tbsp red–wine vinegar
1 lemon (zest only)

RECIPE–SPECIFIC INGREDIENTS: RATATOUILLE

1 eggplant (400 g)
350 g zucchinis
1 yellow and 2 red capsicums
1/4 bunch of basil leaves, with stalks
300 g cherry tomatoes (or conventional tomato)

EQUIPMENT

Enameled cast-iron pot
3 bowls
Bowl for refrigerating capsicum
Blender

PROCESS

Time: approximately 100 minutes.

Activate the barbecue (direct heat, 220 degrees —
lid on).

Peel onion and cut in half.

When barbecue is heated, put onion and all other
vegetables except cherry tomatoes on the grill, whole.

Put cherry tomatoes on flat barbecue plate or in a foil
dish (to avoid them falling through the grill).

When tomatoes begin to shrivel and spurt juice (from
4 to 20 minutes, depending on cooking circumstances —
log for future reference), transfer them to the bowl.

Turn vegetables to achieve 90% blackness on skin
of capsicums and appearance of "cooked" for
remaining vegetables (28 minutes), and process
them as described below. Turn off barbecue.

Cut onion into 8 pieces and put in bowl.

Cut zucchini into 2 1/2 cm discs and put in bowl.

Cut eggplant in half and pull out flesh without
breaking up. Cut each piece lengthwise, then
crosswise to create cubes. Put in bowl.

Allow capsicums to cool (15 minutes, depending
on your tolerance of heat / pain).

Peel capsicums with fingers, cut in half, and discard core and water.

Cut a red capsicum into 2 cm strips; put in bowl; cover with 3 tablespoons of olive oil and 1 tablespoon of red-wine vinegar. Stir, cover, and refrigerate.

Cut remaining capsicums into 2 1/2 cm squares; add to bowl with onions, zucchini, and eggplant.

Tear basil leaves from stalks. Chop stalks into tiny pieces (30 seconds chopping).

Peel and chop garlic (1 minute chopping).

Put pot on burner / hotplate and set temperature to 40% of maximum. Add 2 tablespoons of olive oil, the basil stalks, and the garlic. Fry for 6 minutes.

Add contents of the bowl to the pot, plus 1/2 a teaspoon of salt, 8 turns of the pepper grinder, and 1 tablespoon of balsamic vinegar.

Put lid on pot and adjust heat to simmer for 30 minutes (non-critical).

When ready to eat the Greek gazpacho: put leftover Greek salad in blender with 8 small ice cubes. Blend until smooth. Serve.

When ready to eat the ratatouille: zest a lemon (put remaining lemon in refrigerator for future juicing). Add basil leaves (torn into smaller pieces if very large) and lemon zest on top of ratatouille, and serve.

VARIATIONS

This is a vegan, gluten-free recipe. The former is easily rectified, since the barbecue is already required. Simply add meat of your choice, barbecued as recommended, while the pot is simmering. I recommend merguez sausages or some other form of lamb. Other diners can choose whether they want this addition; the ratatouille can function as a main dish or a side dish. You may want to reduce the quantity.

Jamie Oliver, whose recipe provided the excellent idea of the lemon zest and basil, recommends serving the ratatouille with rice. I disagree — but he is a professional, so you should try it, possibly experimenting with different forms of rice.

SUMMER TUESDAY:

Grilled Figs; Lobster Salad; Cheese and Crackers; Piña-colada Sorbet

Guest night. Quantity for four people.

Recommended cocktail: pink-grapefruit margarita.

Recommended wine: oak-aged sauvignon blanc.

The lobster[1] salad, based on a recipe by Melbourne chef Teage Ezard (inventor of numerous delicious but complex dishes), is a longstanding component of the Standardized Meal System: I served it to Rosie on our first "date." This version has been vastly simplified, primarily through the use of pre-cooked lobster — which may be unavoidable, as live lobsters are difficult to source. This approach also eliminates the risk of traumatic (but conversation-provoking) encounters between guests and their dinner.

Even dead lobster is expensive and the amount specified is the minimum for four persons. Large prawns (shrimp), cooked and peeled, are an excellent alternative. Monkfish is known as "poor man's lobster" and on that basis would seem to be an obvious substitute. Or (refer Variants) you can substitute a cheaper grilled protein and serve the salad "on the side."

For the grapefruit margarita, add an equal quantity[2] of

---

[1] The original recipe is for an Australian *crayfish* — a saltwater crustacean more similar to the Atlantic lobster than the American freshwater crayfish. Seafood naming is notoriously geographically inconsistent and, like much biological naming, based on appearance rather than genetic similarity. Another topic for mealtime discussion.

[2] This is a good starting point. You may wish to add less, possibly as little as zero.

freshly squeezed pink-grapefruit juice to the standard margarita recipe (refer Spring Tuesday). You can top the drink with soda if you or guests prefer it, or if the weather is hot. The drink can then be called a paloma.

COMMON RESOURCES: GRILLED FIGS

Balsamic vinegar

RECIPE-SPECIFIC INGREDIENTS: GRILLED FIGS

4 large or 8 small figs
8 slices prosciutto

COMMON RESOURCES: LOBSTER SALAD

Salad ingredients:
100 g somen noodles
1 tbsp peanut oil
1 tbsp hazelnut oil
1 tbsp tobiko (flying fish roe, frozen product)
1 sheet nori (or 1/2 tbsp green nori sprinkle)
1/2 lemon
Dressing ingredients:
1 egg (yolk only required — I use the white to make a pisco sour to drink while making the salad)
1 tsp Dijon mustard
40 ml Japanese rice-wine vinegar
2 tsp kecap manis (sweet soy sauce)
150 ml peanut oil
1/2 tbsp dried dashi
2 tbsp dried bonito flakes
1/2 lemon (other 1/2 specified in salad ingredients)

RECIPE-SPECIFIC INGREDIENTS: LOBSTER SALAD

1 1/2 kg whole Australian crayfish, cooked, or equivalent lobster, langoustine, or tails of any of these (There is considerable inedible weight in a whole crustacean — in fact, if you are unconcerned about cost, you can double the amount of lobster specified. It will almost certainly be consumed, though you can probably omit the cheese and crackers. If using an alternative sea creature, or tails, seek fishmonger's advice on "how much per person in a salad".)

1 head witlof (Belgian endive / chicory)

1 large mango

1 large avocado or 2 small avocados

COMMON RESOURCES: CHEESE AND CRACKERS

Crackers

RECIPE-SPECIFIC INGREDIENTS: CHEESE AND CRACKERS

Cheese

COMMON RESOURCES: PIÑA-COLADA SORBET

Simple syrup, if needed (standard resource in the cocktail maker's fridge — refer Autumn Tuesday)

RECIPE-SPECIFIC INGREDIENTS: PIÑA-COLADA SORBET

200 g frozen pineapple chunks (frozen on Saturday)

150 ml coconut milk (remainder of can saved from Sunday)

EQUIPMENT

Toothpicks
Serving plates for figs and salad
Scissors for cutting lobster carapace
    (feasible with a knife)
Kettle
Sieve
Blender or food processor
3 bowls (rinse between uses)
Salad bowl
Lemon squeezer
Platter for serving
Small bowl for serving dressing
Chopping board or plate for serving cheese

PROCESS

Time: 31 minutes preparation (after practice).
Minimal time for other tasks.

Start early. The goal is to prepare the figs for cooking and the lobster salad in its entirety before guests arrive (as with any new process, the first time will take much longer). With most of the work done, you will be free to participate in interesting conversations, demonstrate barbecuing confidence, and drink alcohol (optional) with minimal pressure.

Prepare the somen noodles according to the instructions on the packet. Add the peanut oil, toss to coat, and put in refrigerator to cool.

If using large figs, cut them in half lengthwise. Wrap a slice of prosciutto around each fig / half and secure with a toothpick. Figs are "ready to go."

Dissolve the dashi and the bonito flakes in 1 tablespoon of recently boiled water to form a paste. Put in refrigerator.

Extract the crayfish / lobster meat. This is a messy job. You should wear an apron (or clothes that you can wash immediately afterwards — change *before* dinner).

You may want to watch an instructional video on the internet before disassembling a lobster for the first time. Essentially, you need to break off all legs and claws from the body (diners will crack claws and extract the meat themselves), twist the tail off, use scissors to cut the white side of the shell lengthwise, and extract the white "tail" flesh in a single piece. Pull out the thin intestinal tract, which will be within the "head" end of the tail meat.

Wash flesh (the lobster's and your own) to remove tomalley[1] (greenish-brown paste that serves as liver and pancreas). Put lobster legs and claws in a bowl; cover and refrigerate. *Do not put discarded lobster components in the garbage bin unless it is bin-collection night.* It is summer, and they will rapidly decompose and smell terrible. Put in a plastic bag and freeze until bin night.

The messy work is over. A good time to separate the egg and make a pisco sour.

Cut off the base of the witlof and pull the leaves off. Slice each leaf lengthwise into 1/2 cm strips, put in salad bowl, add hazelnut oil, and toss to mix.

---

[1] Some people eat the tomalley but there is a risk of paralytic shellfish poisoning if the lobster has ingested an infected bivalve. Also, many guests are revolted by it, given its texture, color, and function. An interesting topic for conversation.

Make the dressing:

Add egg yolk, mustard, vinegar, and kecap manis to the dashi-bonito paste, and use blender or food processor (preferably) to puree. Still blending / processing, slowly add the peanut oil, *very* slowly at first, then faster until the mixture thickens (you will be familiar with the generic mayonnaise process and repair procedure if you have made Autumn Saturday Dinner; if not, check that day's instructions).

Transfer to a bowl and squeeze the half-lemon in. Stir to mix. Refrigerate.

Slice the lobster tail into 1 1/2 cm discs (plus some untidy remnants) and put in a bowl.

Extract the flesh from the mango and the avocado, and chop into 2 cm cubes. Squeeze the remaining half-lemon over the avocado. Add mango and avocado cubes to the salad bowl. Add the somen noodles. Refrigerate.

If you are using a nori sheet rather than green nori sprinkle, chop the nori sheet into thirds, then each third into 1/2 cm strips 1/3 the length of the original sheet. Breakage is acceptable. Lobster salad is (almost) "ready to go."

Remove cheese from refrigerator.

When guests arrive:

Activate barbecue grill (medium-high). I recommend the gas grill rather than preparing a charcoal fire for such a small task.

When grill is hot, put figs over direct heat. Monitor — they cook quickly.

After 2 minutes (or earlier, if prosciutto shows signs of burning), turn figs over.

After 2 minutes more (or earlier, if prosciutto shows signs of burning), transfer from grill to plate and extinguish grill.

Pour 1/2 a teaspoon of balsamic vinegar over each fig half and serve.

When ready to serve the lobster salad:

Pour over half of the dressing into the salad bowl and mix "gently." Put surplus dressing on table.

Tip the contents of the salad bowl onto the serving platter. Add the lobster pieces on top. Distribute the nori sheet or "sprinkle" on top of the salad. Sprinkle the tobiko on top. Put the lobster legs and claws on the platter beside the salad. Serve.

When ready, serve cheese and crackers.

Sorbet: put pineapple chunks and coconut milk in the blender or food processor and process until the consistency of sorbet. Coconut milk varies in thickness and sweetness. Add simple syrup in increments of 15 ml (1/2 a shot) to sweeten if necessary.

Do not panic if mixture is too liquid the first time: serve as a virgin colada (or add 75 ml of white rum to each serve and serve as actual piña colada — total 2.5 standard drinks). Review your brand of coconut milk or substitute coconut cream — or continue to serve virgin / piña coladas.

Before going to bed, add any lobster shell to the refuse bag in the freezer.

VARIATION

Insert a piece of gorgonzola cheese in each fig before grilling. Include the remainder of the cheese in the cheese course.

If you delete the seafood components — lobster, tobiko, dried bonito flakes, dried dashi — the salad is an excellent accompaniment to grilled protein of any kind. I recommend pork or chicken.

Barbecued Pork with Watermelon Salad; Chocolates

Recommended drink: if there is grapefruit left over from the previous night's margaritas, I make a low-alcohol (less than 1/4 standard drink per person) cocktail. Squeeze a pink grapefruit, shake with 30 ml Campari and 1/3 of a shaker of ice, pour into 2 glasses (including the ice), and top with 60 ml soda. For zero alcohol, replace the Campari with Crodino or other nonalcoholic substitute (some include the soda already).

This is the fifth use of the barbecue in five days, though it plays only a minor role on Saturday and Tuesday. Obviously, it is possible to cook with a single barbecue, just as it is possible to own a single pair of pants. However, the arguments for multiple barbecues are as compelling as those presented to me for extra pants: more options for essentially the same task; backup in case of failure of one; adaptability to different weather. I would add "taking advantage of improvements in technology." And, for the same reasons that *many* people own *vast* numbers of pairs of pants or shoes (sometimes selected because "I just saw them and liked them"), I have several barbecues, including charcoal versions and supporting technology.

For this dish, I recommend either a piece of roasting pork or spareribs. An excellent option for the former is a double or triple pork chop, as the bones add mass, so the meat is less likely to be overcooked by the time the skin is ready.

The situation with spareribs is similar to that with risotto (Spring Wednesday), except that "Italian expert" is replaced by "American expert." Alternatively, you can rely on a butcher who sells pre-marinated ribs. Take their advice on quantity and cooking style, and, as always, revise to reflect experience.

As an alternative to pork, salmon (especially coated in chermoula paste — refer Spring Tuesday) is excellent with the watermelon.

The watermelon salad is adapted from a recipe by Yotam Ottolenghi. If you are unable to purchase a small portion of watermelon, the surplus can be eaten with breakfast[1] or as a post-exercise rehydrating snack.

RECIPE-SPECIFIC INGREDIENTS: BARBECUED PORK

Marinated spareribs suitable for barbecuing,
    as recommended by butcher

or

450 g piece of roasting pork, skin on
    (ask butcher to score the skin)

COMMON RESOURCES: WATERMELON SALAD

15 marinated, pitted black olives
50 g feta cheese (optionally a marinated product)
1 piece of preserved lemon or zest of 1 lemon

RECIPE-SPECIFIC INGREDIENTS: WATERMELON SALAD

250 g watermelon flesh (i.e. excluding skin)
6 basil leaves
8 mint leaves

---

[1] If eating watermelon with breakfast, you could refer to it as "fruit salad." Cafes and hotels routinely serve "fruit salad" consisting entirely of melon.

EQUIPMENT

Serving plate for watermelon salad
Salad servers
Serving plate for pork

If cooking roasting pork:
Kettle
Meat thermometer
Roasting dish for pork

PROCESS

Time: spareribs — according to expert instructions; roast pork — 75 minutes (with significant unallocated time).

In parallel with pork cooking (below) and at any time in the process, make watermelon salad:

Cut watermelon flesh into 1 cm slices (weigh as you proceed), then 4 cm squares. Spread on plate.

Cut olives in half.

Cut preserved lemon or lemon zest into 20 pieces (very small).

Distribute 1 tablespoon of olive oil, feta (cut into 1 cm cubes or crumble with hands), olive halves, preserved lemon, and leaves (each torn into 4 pieces) over watermelon; put on table.

If using spareribs:

Cook on barbecue according to butcher's recommendation.

If using roasting pork:

Remove from refrigerator 30 minutes in advance.

Heat barbecue to 230 degrees, lid on, indirect heat.

Rub 1 tablespoon of salt into pork skin.

Put 1/2 a tablespoon of cooking oil in roasting pan.

Put pork in roasting pan, fat side upwards, and put on barbecue, lid on.

Let pork cook for 25 minutes (skin will blister).

Insert meat thermometer.

When thermometer registers 58 degrees (it may already have exceeded this), turn off barbecue and remove pork to rest for 15 minutes (temperature should reach 63 degrees), then carve / slice.

Serve pork and salad.

Chocolates.

VARIATION

If you require a green vegetable, I recommend green beans, boiled for 10 minutes, rinsed in cold water, then served alongside the watermelon (or replacing the watermelon) with the same topping.

Parmesan Crisps and Prosciutto;
Spaghetti Puttanesca with Green Salad

This meal is not only delicious but could also save your life. It contains a large quantity of salt and I recommend a blood-pressure test for all household members before eating it. If high blood pressure is detected, the physician is likely to be able to prescribe an effective pharmaceutical treatment with (generally) minimal side effects. As well as being able to consume spaghetti puttanesca with relative safety, you will be treating a medical problem which could have had fatal consequences if undetected.

You should also consider a liver-function test before drinking alcohol or continuing to do so. Unfortunately, there is no drug to counteract the short- and long-term negative effects, which may include intoxication and associated antisocial behavior, cancer, and organ failure. I would suggest that the necessary research be crowd-funded. Success would surely represent a major contribution to world health, likely warranting a Nobel Prize.

Until all diners have medical clearance — or if you want some variation from spaghetti puttanesca — I recommend the Major Variant (below). It demonstrates, again, the flexibility of the Standardized Meal System, requiring no change to the shopping list. You can alternate, vote, or randomly select right up to the commencement of cooking.

Parmesan cheese should not be sprinkled on this pasta, because (1) the sauce is oil-based and (2) the sauce contains seafood. Hence the parmesan crisps as an alternative means of including the cheese (note that parmesan is a *salty* cheese).

COMMON RESOURCES: PARMESAN CRISPS

Grana Padano parmesan cheese (Reggiano will work, but is more expensive)

RECIPE-SPECIFIC INGREDIENTS: PARMESAN CRISPS

Prosciutto remaining from Tuesday (approx. 60 g)
100 g marinated capsicums (from Monday's barbecue)

COMMON RESOURCES: SPAGHETTI PUTTANESCA

160 g spaghetti

25 g anchovies

4 cloves garlic

1 tbsp capers (if packed in salt, rinse in a sieve — see preceding note regarding blood pressure)

24 black olives (preferably preserved in oil), pitted — or pit them yourself

1 or 2 birds-eye or alternative preferred chilies, fresh or reconstituted (optional)

RECIPE-SPECIFIC INGREDIENTS: SPAGHETTI PUTTANESCA

14 cherry tomatoes

COMMON RESOURCES: GREEN SALAD

1 tbsp wine vinegar

RECIPE-SPECIFIC INGREDIENTS: GREEN SALAD

75 g green salad leaves
Fresh basil

EQUIPMENT

Grater
1 sheet baking paper or silicone baking mat
Pot for pasta
Frying pan
Bowl
Salad bowl
Jar for shaking vinaigrette
Colander or sieve
Plate for serving parmesan crisps and prosciutto

PROCESS: PARMESAN CRISPS

Time: 22 minutes (largely waiting for oven to heat).

Heat oven to 200 degrees (conventional oven).

Grate cheese into thin, short ribbons to produce
6 tablespoons.

Place grated cheese on baking paper / mat on oven
tray in 4 equal mounds separated by at least 2 cm
(they do not spread as much as might be anticipated).

Cook until they begin to brown (9 minutes).

Remove from oven and allow to cool (3 minutes).
Serve. Trivial!

PROCESS: SPAGHETTI PUTTANESCA AND GREEN SALAD

*Time: approximately 30 minutes, less as you become
better at parallel processing.*

Start the grill or barbecue (maximum temperature,
lid off) and put the cherry tomatoes under / on it.

Monitor the tomatoes. When they have begun to shrivel

and spurt juice (anywhere from 4 to 20 minutes; note for future reference), turn off the barbecue / grill and transfer them to a bowl.

Put leaves in salad bowl. Tear 5 basil leaves from stalks and add to salad bowl.

Put 3 tablespoons of olive oil and the vinegar in jar with 1/4 teaspoon of salt. Put lid on jar (important) and shake vigorously for 15 seconds.

Pour contents of jar on salad and mix with salad serving implements.

Measure 3 tablespoons of olive oil into the frying pan.

Chop the olives into halves, and the chili(es) and garlic into tiny pieces (60 seconds for the garlic, 30 seconds for the chili); add to pan.

Put pan on burner / hotplate at 40% of maximum heat. When the garlic begins to change color (7 minutes[1]), add anchovies, stir to mix, then add olives, capers, chili, and tomatoes (squashing with the wooden spoon). Lower heat to minimum.

Prepare the spaghetti according to instructions on the packet (add 1 tablespoon of salt when the water boils if not specified).

Five seconds before the spaghetti cooking time is reached, transfer 4 tablespoons of the boiling water to the pan, then drain the spaghetti in the colander or sieve, add to the pan, and stir to mix.

Serve in saucepan (or transfer to heated bowl if diners insist).

---

[1] Reminder: *approximate.* Do not allow the garlic to turn black (burn). Reduce heat if necessary.

MAJOR VARIANT: SPAGHETTI WITH PROSCIUTTO, CAPSICUMS, LEMON, AND OLIVES

Do not serve the capsicums or prosciutto with the parmesan crisps. You will need 3 lemons from Common Resources.

Chop olives in half. Put in first bowl, along with capsicums.

Chop prosciutto into strips of approximately 2 x 1/2 cm. Add to bowl.

Chop 10 basil leaves into 6 pieces each (approximately — the leaves can be chopped as a consolidated mass). Add to bowl.

Grate and squeeze the lemons. Add 80 ml of juice to second bowl. If you have surplus juice, refrigerate for another use (e.g. sour cocktail — refer Autumn Tuesday). If you need more, grate and squeeze additional lemons, and add the zest to the first bowl.

Add 160 ml of olive oil, 1/2 a teaspoon of salt, and 8 twists of the pepper grinder to the juice. Stir rapidly with a fork for 10 seconds.

Cook spaghetti according to packet instructions (add 1 tablespoon of salt when the water boils if not specified).

Drain spaghetti and return to pot over minimum heat.

Add the olive oil and juice. Mix with a fork.

Add the contents of the first bowl and mix.

Serve in saucepan (or transfer to heated bowl).

Restaurant Night or Minestrone

Recommended wine: I do not consider wine or cocktails compatible with soup. This may be another motivator to go to a restaurant and eat something different.

COMMON RESOURCES

Frozen minestrone soup
Parmesan cheese
Pesto

EQUIPMENT

Grater

PROCESS

Time: 15 minutes.

Thaw and reheat minestrone soup.

Serve with pesto and parmesan cheese, which diners can add to their individual bowls.

AUTUMN

SATURDAY
Lunch
Deli selection with fresh bread

Dinner
Seafood stew with rustic rouille

SUNDAY
Don's surprise
Ice-cream

MONDAY
Linguini marinara

TUESDAY
(guests)
Tuna sashimi
Thai duck / chicken salad

WEDNESDAY
Mushroom minestrone
Chocolates

THURSDAY
Rice-paper rolls
Stir-fried vegetables

FRIDAY
(if eating at home)
Chili con carne

AUTUMN SATURDAY LUNCH:

Deli Selection with Fresh Bread

Autumn Saturday was at one time the most stressful shopping day in the system, as I needed to purchase unfamiliar ingredients for Don's Surprise on Sunday and spontaneously create an original lunch for Saturday. This was deliberate: I wanted to demonstrate that I could function without the Standardized Meal System. On autumn Saturdays, I simulated the shopping pattern of a less organized person, and, in doing so, reminded myself of how much time and mental effort the system saves.

For Don's Surprise, I had a list of items for the new recipe and could generally obtain them from familiar vendors. The spontaneous lunch was more challenging. I would choose a loaf of bread (olive sourdough), then purchase delicatessen items to accompany it, aiming to produce something I had not served before. But without a shopping list, organized by vendor, the market is overwhelming. Vast numbers of cured meats, marinated vegetables and seafood, dips, cheeses...all with different variations, qualities, and prices.

One autumn Saturday I was examining the selection at a deli when the woman serving noticed my distress. I explained the problem, and she immediately recommended fresh buffalo mozzarella, with tomato and basil from the greengrocer. "Next week I'll have something different for you." This became a pattern — a very satisfactory, win-win solution to my problem.

It was a useful reminder. Learning to work in opposition to one's natural behavior is sometimes necessary, but there is no point in doing so when there are good alternatives, especially ones that let others utilize their strengths.

Retain at least one slice of bread as a dinner ingredient.

Seafood Stew with Rustic Rouille

Recommended cocktail: Americano with absinthe wash.

When our friends Dave and Sonia from New York lived for a time in Melbourne, they insisted on coming to dinner at our house on Saturday instead of Tuesday nights. Rather than further disrupting the week by shifting meals (and in this case impacting on Monday's dinner, which requires tonight's leftovers), I simply scaled up. Sonia commented: "You guys eat a lot of seafood. No wonder you're both so slim."

Sonia was wrong. We eat seafood frequently, but the quantities are no different to the quantities we eat of other food. And eating seafood — especially "a lot of seafood" — does not guarantee a healthy weight. Sonia had fallen into the trap of thinking that a diet based on certain food groups would lead to weight loss, a myth perpetuated by diet books.

The credit should go not to seafood but to the Standardized Meal System, which enables meal sizes to be adjusted precisely to maintain or lose weight at the recommended (slow) pace. Also:

1. My father–in–law Phil's advice on weight management is "don't eat junk." The Standardized Meal System contains minimal "junk" (ice-cream on Autumn Sundays, weekly chocolate), which is carefully regulated. Even these items can be easily eliminated.

2. By following the standardized shopping lists rather than shopping randomly, you will not buy additional junk. If you don't buy junk, you will not have junk available to eat.

3. There is one major exception, which Phil would insist on me pointing out: alcohol, which contains "empty" kilojoules, encourages additional consumption of food and more alcohol, and discourages exercise, as well as being (convincingly) associated with numerous diseases. I recommend not drinking alcohol[1].

4. Regular exercise is important. If you are motivated by quantified goals, I recommend use of a smart watch to monitor exercise (you should already have one for timing cooking activities). It represents vastly better value for money than a prestigious watch with useless "features" (appropriately named *complications*), such as tourbillons.

5. Weigh your body daily. This advice is contrary to conventional wisdom, which mistakenly argues that daily variations can be eliminated by less frequent weighing. It is better to take frequent, regular readings at the same time of day, store them in your monitoring device (see 4), and allow it to create a curve of best fit to show progress.

The rouille is a major factor in the deliciousness of this meal but is incompatible with wine. I suggest an Americano with an optional absinthe (or pastis, such as Pernod or Ricard) rinse: put 10 ml of absinthe in serving glass, tilt to partially coat interior of glass, transfer to next glass until all glasses prepared; drink any remaining. Then make a conventional Americano in those glasses: stir 30 ml of sweet vermouth and 30 ml of Campari

---

[1] Obviously, I have ignored this recommendation, due to its positive effect on my mental health (self-assessed).

with ice; top with 30 ml of soda; garnish with orange slice[1]. Or don't drink alcohol at all.

You will have achieved a low-alcohol or no-alcohol Saturday night[2], which you should not notice due to being distracted by the quality of the meal and the work of extracting seafood from shells. Avoiding alcohol is likely to have more weight-loss benefits than eating seafood.

COMMON RESOURCES: SEAFOOD STEW

1 can tomatoes, 400 g
2 cloves garlic
1 brown onion

RECIPE-SPECIFIC INGREDIENTS: SEAFOOD STEW

This recipe is intended to produce leftovers.

750 g live mussels
12 large raw ("green") prawns (shrimp),
    shelled (tail may still be attached)
1 small calamari, cleaned by fishmonger
6 sea scallops or 12 smaller scallops
1 fillet (250 g) firm fish, as recommended
    by fishmonger for stew or soup
1 hot or mild (smoked) chorizo sausage
1 small fennel bulb

---

[1] If you enjoy the Americano and decide to order it in a bar, be sure to specify Americano *cocktail*, or you are likely to be served a coffee.

[2] Unless you use excessive absinthe for the glass-rinsing process or, in the interests of minimizing waste, use the egg white to make a Boston sour, as I do.

COMMON RESOURCES: RUSTIC ROUILLE

1 egg (use yolk only)
8 cloves garlic (*this is correct*)
2 tsp of peppercorns (white or black)
1 slice bread leftover from lunch, crust removed
2 birds-eye or alternative preferred chilies,
    fresh or reconstituted

EQUIPMENT

Enameled cast-iron pot
Medium bowls
Mortar and pestle
Ladle

PROCESS

*Time: 80 minutes, including significant
unallocated time.*

0: Slice calamari into thin (1 cm or less) rings.

    Remove skin from chorizo and slice chorizo into
    1 1/2 cm discs.

    Put 2 tablespoons of olive oil in pot and heat
    on burner / hotplate (25% of maximum setting).

2: Fry chorizo slices. If they begin to blacken,
    turn them over immediately and reduce heat.

    In parallel with the frying processes, peel onion,
    and chop onion and fennel bulb into 2 cm cubes.

5: Turn over chorizo slices with spatula, if you
    haven't already. If they begin to blacken,
    go immediately to next step.

8: Use spatula to transfer chorizo to bowl, leaving oil from the chorizo in pot, and increase temperature to 80% of maximum.

10: Fry prawns and calamari.

11: Turn over prawns and calamari with spatula.

12: Reduce temperature to 20% of maximum.

Use spatula to transfer prawns and calamari to bowl.

Add onions and fennel to pot. Stir with wooden spoon every 10 minutes.

While onions and fennel are cooking, prepare the rouille:

Put all rouille ingredients except the egg in the mortar, and use the pestle to crush and mix them into a homogenous paste (3 minutes). Alternatively, use the food processor.

Separate egg yolk from white and add yolk to mortar.

Slowly (initially drip by drip[1]) add olive oil to the pestle, stirring rapidly and continuously with a fork, until the mixture thickens to the consistency of mayonnaise, which it is. If it fails to thicken or stops thickening, you will need to perform the oil—egg-emulsion rescue procedure: put another egg yolk in a bowl and add the mixture in the same manner as you should have added the olive oil. You will have another egg white for a cocktail to assist in dealing with the stress of the near–disaster.

Enjoy unallocated time.

60 (non–critical): Increase temperature to 50% of maximum.

---

[1] The rate of pouring should be approximately proportional to the amount of oil in the mortar.

Cut fish into 2 cm cubes. Smell bag of mussels to check for decay (unlikely, but one bad mussel will render the entire meal inedible; smell mussels individually to identify the culprit and remove). Pull "beards" off mussels.

65: Add tomatoes and mussels to pot. Put lid on pot.

70: Remove lid, add contents of bowl and all remaining seafood to pot, and stir contents. Replace lid.

75: Remove lid. If less than 80% of mussels have opened, stir and keep cooking for 5 minutes or until the 80% target is reached.

Using ladle, transfer 1/3 of the stew to the bowl. Cover and refrigerate.

Serve the remaining 2/3 of the stew in the pot. Diners should add rouille (carefully) to their individual servings. Refrigerate leftover rouille.

VARIATIONS

The chorizo is optional but delicious.

The seafood items can be varied to include other bivalves and crustaceans, even to the extent of eliminating the fish.

Convert the stew to a soup by adding 500 ml of commercial fish or shellfish stock with the tomatoes. I recommend deleting the chorizo if you do this. Leave the liquid behind when removing the portion for refrigeration.

If you decide to have a first course (the cooking smells may stimulate hunger), take 1/3 of the prawns, scallops, or calamari, plus 6 slices of chorizo (1 cm each), and fry on the barbecue or in a pan. Their absence from the stew will not be noticed.

AUTUMN SUNDAY:

Don's Surprise; Ice-cream

Common Resource Maintenance
and Advance Preparation:

> Chili con Carne (if necessary)
>
> Chicken Stock (if necessary) —
> refer Summer Sunday for recipe

This day had three major problems.

1. On the occasions when I prepared a batch of chili con carne (for freezing and use on Fridays), it smelled so delicious that Rosie and Hudson insisted on eating a portion of it instead of the standard calf-liver-based meal. *Even if we had eaten chili two days earlier.*

2. When I was not preparing chili, the calf-liver meal was not conducive to concurrent family discussions, due to speed of preparation — and possibly cooking smells.

3. Rosie and Hudson were strongly encouraging me to change this meal.

More generally, the Standardized Meal System needed a process for evolution.

My solution was the non-standard Autumn Sunday. If I am not making chili, I trial a new recipe, based on research, vendor recommendations, or experience in restaurants and friends' homes, sourcing the Recipe-specific Ingredients during my Saturday shopping. In this way I test at least ten new recipes per year, enabling (theoretically) a 36% annual replacement rate.

The dessert is deliberately "indulgent" and trivially easy ("serve ice-cream"), as compensation in the event that the experimental meal is "challenging" to prepare or consume. For the same reason, you may want to serve a familiar pre-dinner cocktail, which can be justified given the reduced alcohol consumption on Saturday. I suggest an Old Fashioned.

COMMON RESOURCE MAINTENANCE: CHILI CON CARNE

The chili con carne recipe makes four double meals (eight serves). It includes zucchini and corn, which are inauthentic[1] but delicious and healthy.

COMMON RESOURCES

4 tbsp chili con carne spice mix
    (commercial product, but preferably
    from specialist spice vendor)
Hot paprika / cayenne pepper
4 cans tomatoes, 400g each
4 cans red kidney beans, 400g each
1 can sweet-corn kernels, 400 g
2 brown onions

RECIPE-SPECIFIC INGREDIENTS

2 red capsicums
400 g zucchini
500 g minced beef

---

[1] Omission of the zucchini will significantly improve the impression of authenticity.

EQUIPMENT

Large enameled cast-iron pot
Bowl
Freezer containers to store meals

PROCESS

*Time: approximately 120 minutes elapsed,
but less than 15 minutes work.*

Remove beef from refrigerator 30 minutes
before next step.

Chop onions into 1 cm cubes.

Chop zucchinis lengthwise into quarters,
then cut crossways into pieces 1 cm thick.

Cut capsicums in half, remove cores, and
cut into 1 cm squares.

Heat 1 tablespoon of oil in pot on burner /
hotplate at 75% of maximum temperature.

Add onions, zucchini, and capsicum, and
cook for 8 minutes, stirring every minute
with spatula, then transfer to bowl.

Increase heat to maximum and add to pot
1/2 a tablespoon of oil, beef, and chili-spice mix.
Cook until meat is uniformly brown (4 minutes),
stirring every minute with spatula, breaking up
any large clusters of mince.

Drain and dispose of liquid from beans and corn.

Add contents of the bowl and the canned
products, and reduce heat to simmer.

After 30 minutes, taste, and progressively add hot pepper (1 teaspoon at a time) to achieve desired level of spice heat.

Continue cooking for between 15 and 90 minutes — non-critical, but the cooking smells are extremely enjoyable.

Serve and eat. Freeze leftovers in meal-size quantities.

VARIATIONS

Interestingly, given the name means "chili with meat", the amount of meat per serve in chili con carne is relatively small and can be reduced further, even to zero, with surprisingly little negative impact on flavor and some positive impact on the number of cow deaths[1] for which you are responsible.

Experiment with the quantity of chili powder, noting advice provided by the vendor.

Add 1 tablespoon of sweet smoked paprika to the spice mix. Obviously, the makers have undertaken considerable research and experimentation to achieve the optimum formula, so this is a personal-taste anomaly, but one which you may share.

[1] As noted in the discussion of Summer Saturday Lunch, the total number of deaths of living creatures is far more difficult to calculate.

Linguini Marinara

Tonight's meal is trivially simple: leftover ("reserved") seafood stew from Saturday reheated and added to linguini.

If you want to add a starter (as I would), I recommend a selection of vegetables cut into slices 1 cm thick (length according to original size of vegetable), grilled on the barbecue and sprinkled with olive oil: vegetable antipasto, consistent with the Italian theme.

COMMON RESOURCES

Leftover seafood stew
160 g linguini

EQUIPMENT

Pot for reheating seafood stew
Pot for cooking linguini

PROCESS

Reheat the seafood over burner at 40% of maximum, with lid on pot. Stir every 5 minutes.

Prepare the linguini as recommended on the packet (add 1 tablespoon of salt when the water boils if not specified), drain, and mix with the reheated seafood.

Serve and put leftover rustic rouille on table to allow diners to stir in whatever quantity they want.

Tuna Sashimi; Thai Duck / Chicken Salad

Guest night. Quantity for four people.

Recommended cocktail: margarita or generic sour.

Recommended wine: white with some sweetness to balance the chili[1] (e.g. pinot gris or gewürztraminer). Or beer.

A margarita is an excellent accompaniment to sashimi, since it contains citrus juice, but any cocktail of the sour family will satisfy this requirement. A sour consists of a base spirit, lemon or lime juice, and a sweetener. Various other flavorings can be added. Vast numbers are published and popular, including the daiquiri (rum), white lady (gin), and whisk(e)y sour (whisk(e)y).

Rather than fill space with minor variations, I have documented the Don Tillman Sour Generator (version for home use only, by persons of legal drinking age):

1. Select base liquor from vodka, gin, tequila, mezcal, white rum, cachaça, any whisk(e)y, dark rum, brandy, pisco, sherry (less alcoholic, less conventional).

2. Select lemon or lime juice.

3. Select sweetener from simple syrup[2], triple sec (e.g. Cointreau), agave syrup (with tequila or mezcal), maple syrup (possibility with whisk(e)y). Sugar can be used directly (e.g. in a caipirinha) but it must be dissolved in the citrus juice.

---

[1] If you don't eat chili, I recommend a dry white wine (unless you prefer sweet wines in general). And, of course, deleting the chili.

[2] Make by heating 1 cup of water with 1 cup of sugar until sugar dissolved. Refrigerate. Store up to one month.

4. Select optional supplementary ingredient (any liqueur or fortified wine or even unfortified wine, vermouth or sherry, Campari, orgeat (almond) syrup, bitters of any kind).

5. Select optional garnish (slice or rind of fruit, maraschino cherry, sprig of mint or another herb).

The formula can be varied, but a starting point is: put 60 ml base liquor, 30 ml juice, 30 ml sweetener, 15 ml supplementary ingredient (two dashes for bitters) in a shaker 1/3 filled with ice. If you want a frothy result, add an egg white. Shake vigorously for at least 45 seconds. Pour. Garnish with garnish. If you want a longer drink, add soda (in which case, don't use egg white).

Document recipe, assess critically, and consider changes to ingredients and amounts. If the cocktail is a success, name it the <Interesting qualifier> <Noun phrase from table below>. If you cannot think of an interesting qualifier related to the ingredients, use your location, e.g. Northcote Mezcalita.

Base liquor	Noun phrase
Vodka	Caprioska
Gin	Lady
Tequila	Margarita
Mezcal	Mezcalita
White rum	Daiquiri
Cachaça	Caipirinha
Whisk(e)y	Whisk(e)y sour
Dark rum	Rum sour
Brandy	Sidecar
Pisco	Pisco sour
Sherry	Sherry[1] sour

---

[1] Or specify the sherry type, e.g. oloroso sour.

The sashimi is trivially easy, but guests are often impressed that you prepare raw fish at home. You should reassure them (with well-researched confidence) that you purchase it from a reliable fishmonger.

Occasionally I have had problems sourcing the sashimi-grade yellowfin (ahi) tuna or the green mangoes. Other forms of tuna, yellowtail (hamachi), or salmon (obviously also "sashimi-grade") can be substituted for the yellowfin. If no suitable fish is available, I suggest purchasing raw ("green") prawns (shrimp) or sea scallops and barbecuing them — simple and delicious.

The green mango can be replaced by green papaya or ripe mango (in the latter case, cut into 1 1/2 cm cubes rather than strips).

COMMON RESOURCES: SASHIMI

Soy sauce
Prepared wasabi (typically sold in tube)

RECIPE-SPECIFIC INGREDIENTS: SASHIMI

1 thick slice "sashimi-grade" yellowfin tuna (200 g)

COMMON RESOURCES: THAI DUCK SALAD

100 g tamari almonds (or non-tamari almonds, cashews, or peanuts)
For dressing:
1 tbsp tahini
Limes (for juice)
2 tsp maple syrup
80 ml soy sauce
1 birds-eye or alternative preferred chili, fresh or reconstituted (optional)

RECIPE–SPECIFIC INGREDIENTS: THAI DUCK SALAD

700 g duck fillets
250 g zucchini
1 red capsicum
1 yellow capsicum
1 long green chili
1 bunch spring onions
2 green mangoes
1/2 packet bean shoots
1 bunch coriander

EQUIPMENT

Bowl
Serving plates for sashimi and salad
Small bowls / plates for serving soy sauce
    and wasabi (preferably 1 per person)
Jar for mixing dressing
Meat thermometer

PROCESS

*Time: 55 minutes, including time to greet guests
and make cocktails.*

Preferably before guests arrive, prepare salad:

Squeeze limes to produce 40 ml of juice. Put juice in jar
with other dressing ingredients and shake to amalgamate.

Cut capsicums, zucchini, and long chili into 1 cm strips.
Halve strips as necessary to achieve a more consistent
length. Put in bowl with bean shoots.

Tear the coriander leaves from their stalks and add
to bowl.

Chop chili into tiny pieces (30 seconds) and edible part of spring onions into 3 mm discs, and add both to bowl.

Take enough salad to fill 2 rice-paper rolls, put in a container, and refrigerate.

Peel green mango / green papaya using a vegetable peeler and cut into thin strips to match the zucchini strips. (If using a ripe mango, slice into 4 "cheeks" around the stone; use a knife to mark out 1 cm cubes, cutting from the flesh side but not into the skin — a crisscross pattern; turn cheeks inside out; cut away cubes from skin.)

Add mango and the nuts to the bowl containing the chopped / sliced vegetables.

Fifteen minutes before guests are due[1]:

Activate barbecue (indirect heat, lid on).

When barbecue reaches 180 degrees, put poultry on barbecue, skin side down, for 5 minutes.

When timer sounds, turn poultry over and set timer for 15 minutes.

Slice sashimi into the thinnest possible intact slices, observing the general carving rule to cut across the grain. Arrange on serving plate. Put 30 ml of soy sauce and 1 teaspoon of wasabi in each small bowl.

When guests arrive, make cocktails and serve sashimi (traditionally eaten with chopsticks).

---

[1] I recommend use of the word "sharp" when specifying arrival time, and the avoidance of such ambiguous formulations as "6:30 for 7:00." If you have French guests, it is vital to emphasize that local custom is for guests not to be "politely late." If you are French yourself, you should expect guests from other countries to arrive at the time you specify, and therefore you should be clothed and prepared.

When timer sounds, use meat thermometer to test poultry for doneness and cook longer if necessary, taking into account that temperature will rise 5 degrees during "resting." When required temperature is reached, turn off barbecue and allow poultry to rest for 15 minutes (lid on).

Pour dressing into bowl containing the chopped / sliced vegetables; mix with a fork and pour contents of bowl onto salad serving plate.

Slice poultry (across grain) into pieces 1 cm thick. Isolate sufficient to fill 2 rice-paper rolls when chopped and add to container in refrigerator. Put remainder of poultry on top of salad. Serve when diners are ready.

VARIATIONS

Sear the entire piece of tuna for 1 minute each side over maximum heat on the barbecue before slicing. Optionally, rub with olive oil and chili salt before doing so (highly recommended).

Instead of serving the sashimi with wasabi and soy (which is simple and excellent), experiment with lime / lemon juice, with or without added soy, poured over, and chopped garlic, chilies, and capers in any combination.

None of the salad ingredients except the mango / papaya are critical — you can experiment with deleting, replacing, or supplementing them with other vegetables, nuts, etcetera. Chicken (note higher internal temperature target[1]), or other meat or seafood, can replace the duck.

---

[1] Do not rely on the picture of a duck or chicken on the meat thermometer. Correct temperatures are 52 degrees (duck) and 74 degrees (chicken).

AUTUMN WEDNESDAY:

Mushroom Minestrone; Chocolates

This is a "light" meal, though obviously any meal can be made heavier by cooking and eating more of it. The quantity specified is intended to satisfy two adults and the Standardized Meal System allows the amount to be precisely tuned. But it is insufficient for four persons.

The mushroom minestrone was scheduled when Rosie arrived home with her boss, Judas, and colleague, Stefan, as unexpected guests (unexpected because I had not checked my text messages in the preceding 57 minutes — checking for communications more often than hourly is a serious distraction).

My initial thought was that an inadequate meal would discourage such behavior in future. Also, Rosie constantly complains about Judas and Stefan, so it seemed there was no need to give them an undeserved high-quality meal.

As often happens, my judgment of the personal dynamics and / or appropriate response was incorrect. Rosie indicated to me that she would like me to "ramp it up" and "show them what we can do." It seemed that I was being asked to weaponize food — again.

The subject had previously been discussed in relation to regular guest nights. It is conventional to cook more elaborate meals when guests are invited, but Rosie had sought to dissuade me from doing so, observing that our guests were intimidated by the complexity of the dishes, which they would feel obliged to match if they invited us to their homes in return.

She said, "Becca's *afraid* to have us for dinner because you're such a good cook." Obviously, it is flattering to have one's expertise recognized. And if Becca is an incompetent cook, eating at her home could be unpleasant or unsafe, as well as (demonstrably) anxiety-provoking for Becca. Dining at other people's homes is always stressful: the typically excessive number of guests, the host distracted and agitated by attempting a too-complex meal, the awkward and time-wasting protocols for leaving.

"Becca says she'll have to buy us dinner at a restaurant instead," said Rosie.

Perfect outcome. Hence, retention of the elaborate-food-for-guests principle. And the Standardized Meal System allows for the complexity (and heaviness) of any meal to be increased at short notice. With minimal effort, I can add mixed antipasto (olives, preserved goods, salumi); cheese and nuts; and fresh fruit (or, since it was autumn, affogato — ice-cream with an espresso coffee[1] and a shot of amaretto) and chocolates (already specified for Autumn Wednesday) with Pedro Ximenes sherry, all from Common Resources.

In this case, I included all of these, plus a further course, employing my general solution to any problem which renders the scheduled main course nonviable (e.g. inability to shop or a fault in a critical ingredient). The key element of the emergency-food solution is pasta, supplemented with other Common Resources.

---

[1] Obviously, if you don't drink coffee in the evenings, omit the coffee. Reactions to coffee vary, and you should be aware of yours, unless you have made a decision not to drink it at all.

Example pasta flavorings include:

Oil, garlic and chili

Parmesan cheese and butter

Anchovies (simple but surprisingly good)

Puttanesca (except in summer, when it is Monday's meal)

Pizzaiola (in winter, if this option is selected, it is then necessary to eat at a restaurant on Friday or have the same meal twice)

I decided on spaghetti puttanesca (possibly subconsciously hoping that Judas had high blood pressure), omitting the tomatoes due to lack of tomatoes, and serving it as a main course after the soup.

Meanwhile, I delegated Rosie to make negronis to dull our guests' critical faculties and to assist me in dealing with the change to routine. If I had not had an expert cocktail maker available, I would have served good-quality red vermouth on ice with a curl of orange zest.

Except for the (now widely accepted) practice of serving pasta as a main course rather than before it, I had created a reasonably authentic Italian meal. Due to the pasta, it was necessary to open a bottle (technically, two bottles) of red wine. Judas and Stefan were highly impressed, and it was probable that their sleep was disturbed by the combination of alcohol, coffee, and salt.

The negroni should be made according to the International Bartenders Association recipe: equal quantities of gin, good-quality sweet vermouth, and Campari. (The vermouth and Campari should be stored in the fridge, and the gin in the freezer with the glasses.)

Stir over ice, and serve with the ice and a slice of orange. It is fashionable to serve a negroni with a single large ice cube — this will not dilute the drink as much but will be less effective in maintaining coldness, and *coldness is critical*.

COMMON RESOURCES

10 g dried porcini (or alternative
    interesting) mushrooms
1 clove garlic
500 ml chicken stock (from Sunday)
1 can cannellini beans, 400 g
1 bay leaf
Parmesan cheese, for grating over soup

RECIPE-SPECIFIC INGREDIENTS

25 g prosciutto (optional[1])
180 g fresh interesting mushrooms
    (conventional mushrooms are acceptable)
1 leek
2 tbsp flat-leaf parsley (measured
    after chopping; optional)
200 g zucchini

EQUIPMENT

Enameled cast-iron pot
Ladle for serving
Bowl
Jar
Grater

---

[1] Rosie considers that the prosciutto "makes the soup taste like coq au vin without the coq or the vin but not in a bad way." This is probably true.

PROCESS

Time: 50 minutes, including 30 minutes unallocated time.

Put dried mushrooms in jar and add hot water (not boiling) to original level of mushrooms (some mushrooms will float). Shake jar (with lid on) to ensure soaking.

Cut prosciutto into 2 cm squares.

Chop mushrooms into 1 1/2 cm cubes — this is *very* approximate; if you have small mushrooms, leave them whole.

Cut leek (stop when you reach the tough leaves) and zucchini into 1 cm discs.

Cut garlic into tiny pieces (30 seconds chopping).

Heat 1 1/2 tablespoons of olive oil in pot at maximum temperature.

Add prosciutto to pot and cook until crisp (2 minutes).

Reduce heat to 70% of maximum.

Add fresh mushrooms to pot and cook for 4 minutes (stir with wooden spoon after 2 minutes).

Add leek, zucchini, and garlic to oil, and cook for 10 minutes.

While the vegetables cook, drain liquid from cannellini beans (discard liquid).

Add stock (you can preheat in microwave to speed process), dried mushrooms with the soaking water, cannellini beans, and bay leaf to pot. Put lid on.

Simmer for 30 minutes (no intervention required beyond monitoring simmer; if diners are not ready, it can be left to simmer until they are — assuming same evening).

Chop parsley. Put grater, parmesan cheese, and parsley on table. Remove bay leaf from pot.

Serve soup.

Chocolates.

AUTUMN THURSDAY:

Rice-paper Rolls; Stir-fried Vegetables

I consider the most important factor in the success of a relationship (life partnership, friendship, possibly parenting) to be the initiation, planning, and execution of *joint projects*. Humans are cooperative animals, and cooperation is intrinsically satisfying. Identifying interesting projects relies on a mutual understanding of capabilities, needs, and ambitions — a process which requires and promotes *empathy*[1].

The planning of joint projects is the perfect conversation topic — and you are unlikely to be accused of monologuing, since the other person is a "stakeholder." Carrying out the projects may be less exciting and important to the relationship than the planning, but it promotes interaction and fulfills one of the obvious goals of a relationship: spending time together.

Joint projects need to be supported by a policy of tolerance and forgiveness. Errors are inevitable in tackling challenging projects (including the ongoing project of the relationship itself).

I consider this vital information, but I am accustomed to being atypical, so it may not apply to you. Nevertheless, I suggest you reflect on it, and on what you can do to improve your personal implementation of it, while preparing rice-paper rolls and stir-fried vegetables.

---

[1] Empathy is frequently mischaracterized as arising only from intuition. In my experience, empathy can also be achieved (and often more accurately) by interrogation and discussion.

COMMON RESOURCES: RICE-PAPER ROLLS

4 rice-paper-roll wrappers
1 tbsp soy sauce
1 lime
1 tbsp toasted sesame oil
1/2 tbsp fish sauce
1 birds-eye or alternative preferred chili, fresh
    or reconstituted (optional)

RECIPE-SPECIFIC INGREDIENTS: RICE-PAPER ROLLS

Leftover duck and Thai salad
1 tsp chopped spring onion

COMMON RESOURCES: STIR-FRIED VEGETABLES

3 cloves garlic
1 1/2 cm cube of fresh ginger (with experience,
    you may decide to increase this)
2 birds-eye or alternative preferred chili, fresh
    or reconstituted (optional)
3 tbsp hoisin sauce
3 tbsp soy sauce
2 small carrots, cut into matchstick-sized pieces

RECIPE-SPECIFIC INGREDIENTS:
STIR-FRIED VEGETABLES

100 g baby sweet corn
6 spring onions
1 red pepper
100 g mushrooms
1 bunch broccolini *or* 200 g broccoli *or*
    200 g snow peas *or* 1 medium zucchini

EQUIPMENT

Jar for mixing
Lemon squeezer
Bowl
Bowl for dipping sauce
Wok
Dish for soaking rice–paper–roll wrappers

PROCESS

Time: 28 minutes.

If you have neither wrapped a rice–paper roll nor seen it done, I recommend googling an instructional video. It should be simple after the first time (you should ensure you have spare wrappers on that occasion).

Squeeze the lime.

Chop the chili into tiny pieces (30 seconds).

Chop the spring onion into 1/2 cm discs to create 1 1/2 teaspoons of chopped onion.

Put the lime juice, soy sauce, sesame oil, and fish sauce in the jar, and shake vigorously (lid on) for 10 seconds. Pour into serving bowl. Add chili and spring onion to float on top.

Chop the leftover duck and salad into 1 cm cubes where feasible. Mix together in bowl with the chili and spring onions, then divide into 4 equal portions.

Put the roll wrappers in a dish and cover with water — press them under if necessary. When pliable (2 minutes), pull one out and, on the chopping board, place a portion of the duck mix on it. Wrap according to past experience or recent tuition. Or "figure it out."

Serve with the dipping sauce, then dismiss the other diner(s) while you prepare the stir-fried vegetables.

Peel garlic and ginger. Chop them and the chili into small pieces (30 seconds chopping each).

Prepare all remaining vegetables in advance to avoid stress. Use the baby sweet corn as your size reference (cut a 7 x 1.2 cm piece of another vegetable if you have substituted the corn with another vegetable — if the corn is longer than 8 cm, cut in half). Cut all vegetables to that size. *Approximately*.

Put 2 tablespoons of cooking oil in wok on heat source and set temperature to maximum.

When oil is smoking, add the spring onions, garlic, ginger, and chili; stir for 1 minute.

Reduce heat to 70%.

Add vegetables according to the timeline below and stir while they fry (hence the term "stir fry"; you don't need to stir while you are performing the vegetable-adding task).

- 0: Mushrooms.
- 2: Carrot, capsicum, and sweet corn.
- 5: Green vegetable(s).
- 10: Hoisin and soy sauce.

Cook for a further 2 minutes or until all the vegetables are cooked but not too soft.

VARIATIONS

The rice-paper rolls can be deep or shallow fried (set burner / hotplate to 75%) in cooking oil. Let them dry before cooking. Less healthy but more delicious.

Use (smaller) spring-roll wrappers and deep fry.

Add grated ginger to the rolls.

The stir-fry recipe is readily adapted to a vast number of different vegetables (though I recommend avoiding root vegetables).

You can add red meat, poultry, or seafood to the stir fry in place of one or more vegetables. I recommend giving it first place in the cooking sequence.

Buy hoisin noodles and cook according to instructions on pack. Add to wok after final vegetables and stir to mix.

Serve rice (of your preferred variety) with the stir-fried vegetables.

AUTUMN FRIDAY:

Restaurant Night or Chili con Carne

Recommended alcohol: beer.

Do not buy avocados! Discipline begins with shopping. If you have the potential to make guacamole (and to eat it with corn chips or broken taco shells), you will sabotage any possibility of eating out. Guacamole is the perfect accompaniment to chili con carne and margaritas are the logical accompaniment to guacamole. A meal of this deliciousness will be impossible to resist. Just reheat the chili con carne. Or go out.

VARIATIONS:

(Do not read unless you are definitely not going out.)

Put the chili into taco shells. Top with cheese. Heat in oven.

Make nachos: put corn chips in oven dish; top with the chili, hot sauce (optional), and cheese; heat in oven.

Buy avocados and make guacamole. Add it to nachos, above. Make margaritas. Congratulate yourself for resisting being bullied.

WINTER

SATURDAY
Lunch
Toasted cheese

Dinner
Oysters natural
Baked fish with olives and feta

SUNDAY
Jerusalem artichoke soup
Slow-cooked lamb shanks with celeriac mash

MONDAY
Potato and leek soup

TUESDAY
(guests)
Jerusalem artichoke soup
Gougères
Coq au vin with roasted broccoli

WEDNESDAY
Lentil stew
Chocolates

THURSDAY
Poppadums
Chicken curry

FRIDAY
(if eating at home)
Fusilli pizzaiola

Toasted Cheese

One of the many unreasonable criticisms of the Standardized Meal System is that it is not sufficiently "healthy." Today's lunch, which consists largely of wheat and fat, is likely to provoke such comments. The people making the criticism are probably (a) not examining the meal in the context of the full week's menu; (b) relying on unscientific ideas (the bread contains gluten, which is not harmful unless you have an intolerance); and (c) unable to provide evidence that their own eating regimen is better — not even able to produce a week's summary.

People who choose to do something in an organized (or unconventional) manner are held to a higher standard than people who do not. The Standardized Meal System is not provably perfect, but it is almost certain to be healthier than most people's semi-random and fad-influenced diets.

In fact, this meal is intended to improve *mental* health, as it prompts happy memories of my mother cooking cheese on toast for weekend and holiday lunches. You may wish to substitute some other meal with similar effects.

Also, any meal I cook is likely to be healthier than Dave's Diabetic Breakfast (named because it was likely a contributor to his Type 2 diabetes), which he was eating *every day*. (Brush bacon with maple syrup[1] and cook in oven until crisp. Fry eggs, potatoes, and optionally black

---

[1] The use of the imperative form should not be interpreted as an instruction to follow Dave's example. The result is, however, delicious, with the exception of the coffee if you are accustomed to black and unsweetened.

---

pudding and mushrooms in butter. Eat with white bread and jam, and white coffee with sugar.)

COMMON RESOURCES

Generic "cheddar" cheese

RECIPE-SPECIFIC INGREDIENTS

Bread

PROCESS

Time: 10 minutes.

Activate grill. Slice 2 slices of bread (if not already sliced) — more, if the bread cross-section is small or you are hungry.

Slice sufficient cheese to cover the bread. Do not put it on the bread yet.

Place bread under grill until slightly colored (light brown).

Remove bread from grill, turn over, and add cheese to untoasted side to cover. Place under grill until cheese bubbles.

Turn off grill. Remove and serve.

VARIATIONS

Spread butter and / or yeast extract (Vegemite) on the bread immediately before adding cheese. Alternatively — as preferred by Hudson — spread the yeast extract (carefully, in order not to break the thin cheese crust) over the cooked product.

Upgrade to full double-slice toasted sandwiches made in a commercial device, and / or add traditional toasted-sandwich ingredients such as tomato and ham.

WINTER SATURDAY DINNER:

Oysters Natural;
Baked Fish with Olives and Feta

Recommended alcohol: for the oysters, I recommend a Chablis or unoaked sauvignon blanc.

With the fish: rosé or a light red wine, as it is winter, the dish has strong flavors, and I like red wine.

Many people do not like oysters. *Most* people have an aversion to some food or taste: sea urchin, sea cucumbers, jellyfish, snails, coriander, yogurt, olives, anchovies, cauliflower, milk, tomalley. I recommend you reflect on the food you find most distasteful and imagine being forced to eat it.

As an adult, you are unlikely to be faced with this scenario. But when I was a child, I was required to eat things I didn't like, on the basis that I would get used to them, suffer malnutrition without them, or even that I was somehow contributing to world hunger. These arguments were without merit. As an adult, my tastes have changed, but not because of forced exposure.

If you don't like something, I recommend you delete it from the menu (I assume you will do that even without my advice). If your child or someone in your power such as an elderly parent does not like something, I recommend you do the same. Not to do so would demonstrate a severe lack of *empathy*, which is generally regarded as a major character fault.

On the topic of empathy, it is unlikely that oysters feel pain. Also, I was told that opening an oyster kills it immediately — hence the advice to purchase them unshucked. As a result of doing so, I injured my knee[1]. The advice was faulty. You should not eat a dead oyster (you can test for decay by smelling). But I now purchase oysters from a vendor who I trust to have shucked them very recently, and eat them the same day.

COMMON RESOURCES: OYSTERS

2 lemons

RECIPE–SPECIFIC INGREDIENTS: OYSTERS

12 fresh oysters in shells

COMMON RESOURCES: BAKED FISH WITH OLIVES AND FETA

1 lemon
18 pitted black olives
100 g feta cheese (optional)
1 tbsp capers
50 ml white / rosé wine (optional — if you are not drinking white or rosé wine, delete; the flavor contribution is minimal and red wine will have a negative impact)

RECIPE–SPECIFIC INGREDIENTS: BAKED FISH WITH OLIVES AND FETA

350 g fish fillet(s) suitable for baking with tomatoes and olives (as recommended by fishmonger)
14 cherry tomatoes or 1 large conventional tomato

---

[1] The Oyster Shucking Incident is described in the opening chapter of *The Rosie Result*.

EQUIPMENT

Plate for serving oysters
Baking dish with lid
Zester or grater
Plate for lemon zest
Bowl
Lemon squeezer

PROCESS

Time: 37 minutes, including 25 minutes unallocated time.

Heat oven or barbecue to 190 degrees.

Zest and squeeze 1 lemon.

Cut cherry tomatoes in half (or conventional tomato into pieces of this size).

Use knife to "crumble" feta (10 seconds chopping).

Put 3 tablespoons of olive oil in baking dish.

Put fish in baking dish.

Add white wine.

In sequence, put tomatoes, olives, capers, feta, lemon zest, lemon juice, and 1 tablespoon of olive oil on top of the fish.

Put lid on dish, place in oven, and set timer for 25 minutes.

Cut 2 lemons into 4 wedges each. Put the oysters on a plate with them. Ensure a pepper grinder is on the table. Eat oysters.

When timer sounds, serve the fish.

VARIATIONS

Add toppings to the oysters: for example, 1 tablespoon of soy sauce, 1 tablespoon of vinegar, 1 teaspoon of sesame oil (mixed).

Cook the oysters using the "Kilpatrick" recipe. This recipe provides "something for everyone": Worcestershire sauce for me, bacon for Dave, oyster death for Rosie.

Replace the fish with raw ("green") prawns (shrimp).

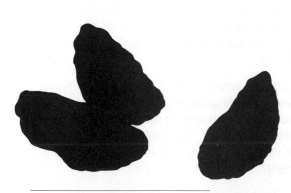

Slow-cooked Lamb Shanks with Celeriac Mash

Common Resource Maintenance
and Advance Preparation:

> Jerusalem Artichoke Soup for Tuesday
> (and tonight)
>
> Coq au Vin for Tuesday (it will be
> improved by reheating)
>
> Potato and Leek Soup (if required)
>
> Chicken Stock (if required) —
> refer Summer Sunday for recipe

Sunday meal preparation is *intended* to be time-consuming. Thanks to standardization, the work imposes only a small cognitive load. As familiarity improves, you will be able to process recipes in parallel, but if today's list (including tonight's meal of Lamb Shanks, which is relatively simple) provokes anxiety, defer the Jerusalem Artichoke Soup until tomorrow or Tuesday, or delete altogether. The advantage of making it today is that you can eat some as an appetizer tonight.

When I was single, Sunday cooking provided an opportunity to prepare mentally for the week ahead. But, following my incorporation into a family, it serves a second function.

My mother spent considerable time in the kitchen when I was young, and my siblings and I would join her to assist, and to talk about random issues. In retrospect, these issues were often important, but would not have been volunteered in response to the conventional question "How was school?"

I realized that I should provide the same service to Hudson and even Rosie. In theory, shared meals are a forum for conversation, but I find that personal matters are better discussed and solutions workshopped during the preparation phase.

Hence the kitchen and barbecue function as conceptual help desks, particularly on Sundays. Frequently, Hudson or Rosie will approach me as I work, knowing that the routine of cooking is likely to have made me even more calm and rational than I am by default, and engage in discussion. Important information is shared and solutions explored.

If I am not required for that task, I have little trouble filling the time with reflection on my own problems. A kitchen with food cooking is an excellent personal environment during the winter (equivalent to a barbecue in fine weather).

SLOW-COOKED LAMB SHANKS

COMMON RESOURCES: LAMB SHANKS

2 tbsp plain flour
2 brown onions
3 carrots
2 cloves garlic
100 ml white wine (can be replaced by extra chicken stock)
100 ml homemade chicken stock (can be replaced by extra wine)
25 g anchovies preserved in oil

RECIPE-SPECIFIC INGREDIENTS: LAMB SHANKS

Sufficient lamb shanks for 2 people (sizes vary, so seek advice from butcher or make your own estimate of how much is required by imagining half of the quantity on your own plate)

Large sprig of rosemary

2 sticks of celery

1 leek

COMMON RESOURCES:
POTATO AND 60% CELERIAC MASH

140 g potatoes

210 g (peeled weight) celeriac (treated as a Common Resource — a celeriac bulb is usually 420 g or larger, but it will last a week in cling wrap in the refrigerator after cutting)

3 cloves garlic

EQUIPMENT

Enameled cast-iron pot or slow cooker

Potato masher

Pot for boiling potatoes and celeriac

Colander

Plate

Plastic bag

PROCESS

Time: 4 hours in pot or 6 hours (check instructions) in slow cooker, mostly unallocated time.

You can cook the lamb shanks in either the cast-iron pot or a specialized slow cooker. If using the latter, the instructions for it should override mine and you will probably need to start earlier.

If you have limited preparation time, you can ignore the frying steps, delete the olive oil, and just put all ingredients in the pot (after peeling, chopping, and removing from packaging, obviously), then commence the main cooking process. The result will still be excellent, but you will miss the therapeutic value of the chopping and sautéing (the procedure is similar to that for minestrone soup and the same observations apply).

Put lamb shanks in bag with flour, 1 teaspoon of salt, and 8 twists of the pepper grinder. Shake.

Put 2 tablespoons of olive oil in cast-iron pot on burner / hotplate and set temperature to maximum.

When hot, put the lamb shanks in the pot and turn as necessary until brown on all sides. If the flour begins to burn, discontinue the process immediately.

Remove lamb shanks to plate. If there is burnt residue in the pot, clean it before proceeding.

Peel onions and chop into 1 cm cubes.

Peel garlic and chop into pieces (30 seconds).

Reduce temperature to 60% of maximum and put 2 more tablespoons of olive oil in the pot.

Add the chopped onions and garlic to the pot.

Preheat the oven to 180 degrees.

In sequence, prepare each of the remaining vegetables, add to those already in the pot, and stir with wooden spoon. Timing is non-critical.

Carrots — peel and cut into discs 1 cm thick.

Leek — discard tough parts and cut into 1 cm discs.

Celery — cut into 1 cm slices.

Add the anchovies (each chopped into 3 equal pieces), rosemary, wine, and chicken stock; stir to mix, then return the lamb shanks to the pot.

Put the lid on the pot, place it in the oven, and reduce the temperature to 165 degrees.

Non-essential step: after 2 hours, remove pot from oven, remove lid, turn lamb shanks over, and replace in oven with lid on.

After 3 1/2 hours the lamb should be ready to serve.

Thirty minutes before serving: remove lid from cast-iron pot (non-essential).

Peel potato(es) with peeler and cut skin from celeriac with knife. Cut both into 3 cm cubes.

Put pieces in pot; cover with cold water and 2 teaspoons of salt.

Put pot on burner / hotplate at maximum. When the water boils, lower heat to maintain simmer for 25 minutes.

Peel garlic cloves and cut finely (1 minute).

Strain vegetables in colander. Return them to the pot, add olive oil and garlic, and mash with potato masher. Serve in saucepan unless diners object.

Serve lamb shanks in cast-iron pot. Sometimes the vegetables will have become a bit fatty. The vegetables have done their primary job of transferring flavor to the meat and can be ignored, but if it is a problem, I suggest steaming a green vegetable.

VARIATIONS

This recipe is tolerant of time (more rather than less), ingredients, and quantities. You can add further seasoning (e.g. chili flakes, coriander) to the flour mixture, and any root vegetable, a can of tomatoes, and / or chili to the pot.

This is a generic casserole recipe, and the lamb shanks can be replaced with any meat suitable for slow cooking: I recommend beef cheeks (minimum of 4 hours cooking; delete the rosemary and anchovies).

The ratio of celeriac to potato can be varied according to taste and the size of the celeriac to avoid wastage (potatoes can be stored longer than celeriac and are less expensive).

ADVANCE PREPARATION: JERUSALEM ARTICHOKE SOUP

This recipe makes six small serves — two for tonight and four for Tuesday. It can easily be scaled up and the surplus frozen, if chicken-stock stocks are sufficient and you have time to peel artichokes. (If a helper is available, delegate them to do this and purchase enough for the remainder of the season.)

COMMON RESOURCES

500 ml homemade chicken stock
Butter

RECIPE-SPECIFIC INGREDIENTS

400 g Jerusalem artichokes
2 leeks

EQUIPMENT

Enameled cast-iron pot
Blender / liquidizer
Colander

PROCESS

Time: 2 1/2 hours, largely unallocated time.

Peel the artichokes (a slow process, due to the shape of the artichokes; it may help to cut off the most irregular shapes and peel them separately).

Cut the artichokes into thin slices (as thin as possible while keeping the slices whole — not critical) and put in colander.

Sprinkle 3 tablespoons of salt over the artichoke slices and toss with hands to ensure most surfaces are coated.

Leave in sink or over a bowl (to catch liquid) for 1 hour.

Discard the liquid that has run off and rinse the artichoke slices to (largely) eliminate the salt.

Dry the artichoke slices with paper towel(s) or clean tea towel(s). Do not spend more than five minutes on this task: perfection is impossible and unnecessary.

Cut leeks from white end into 1 cm discs until you reach the tough part. Discard remainder.

Put olive oil, butter, and leeks in pot, and cook at 25% of maximum for 30 minutes.

Add the chicken stock. Raise temperature to maximum until stock reaches simmer, then lower to maintain simmer. Simmer for 30 minutes.

Allow soup to cool for 15 minutes, then process in blender until smooth. It will be thick — this is correct. Reheat and eat immediately, or put in refrigerator for reheating tonight and Tuesday. Freeze any quantity surplus to those requirements.

ADVANCE PREPARATION: COQ AU VIN

As indicated by the word *vin*, wine is a critical ingredient in coq au vin. Burgundy, specifically Chambertin, is recommended, but not by me:

1. Many people would be unable to identify the subtle differences between Chambertin and generic Burgundy or even Australian pinot noir, when presented under ideal tasting conditions.

2. I predict that *nobody* would be able to detect reliably the differences after the wines had been boiled for 90 minutes with chicken, bacon, shallots, garlic, flour, salt, and pepper.

3. The properties that make a wine superior for drinking are unlikely to be the properties that make it superior for cooking.

4. Chambertin is extremely expensive. If you can afford it and appreciate its qualities, you would surely not pour it into the chicken pot.

Hence, I recommend generic red wine of the minimum standard that you are prepared to drink. Obviously, you should verify this before using. It does not need to be pinot noir, and in fact heavier wines such as shiraz / syrah may give a better result[1].

---

[1] This is an impression I have formed, but I have not had the time to do a double-blind trial. My sole substandard outcome was with a very light pinot noir, but it is possible there were other factors which I did not observe.

COMMON RESOURCES

3 tbsp plain flour

3 cloves garlic

12 shallots

RECIPE-SPECIFIC INGREDIENTS

4 chicken Marylands (drumstick and thigh together
or disassembled), skin removed by vendor, total
weight 900 g

200 g smoked lardons or lean bacon (cut 1 cm thick)

300 g button mushrooms

250 ml pinot noir or other red wine

EQUIPMENT

Enameled cast-iron pot

PROCESS

Time: 3 hours, including substantial unallocated time.

Peel all shallots.

Chop bacon into 1 cm cubes.

Grind pepper over chicken — six 90-degree twists
each side of each Maryland.

Peel garlic and chop into small pieces (30 seconds
chopping).

0: Pour 10 ml of olive oil into pot; place on burner /
    hotplate at 75% of maximum temperature.

2: Add bacon to pot.

5: Stir bacon with spatula.

8: With spatula, transfer bacon to bowl and add
    10 ml of oil to pot.

9: Add shallots to pot.

12: Stir shallots with spatula to expose uncooked surface to heated oil.

15: With spatula, transfer shallots to bowl; then add 10 ml of oil to pot.

17: Add mushrooms to pot.

20: Stir mushrooms with spatula to expose uncooked surface to heated oil.

23: Transfer mushrooms to bowl and add 10 ml of oil to pot.

24: Put flour on chopping board and dip in chicken to coat both sides of all pieces; add surplus flour to bowl and stir with wooden spoon.

25: Add chicken to pot. Place to maximize contact with oil.

30: Use spatula to turn all chicken pieces over (they should be brown — if not, cook them until they are).

35: Transfer chicken pieces to bowl (they should be brown on both sides — if not, cook them until they are).

37: Add wine to pot and use spatula to scrape residue from surface of pot.

38: Add contents of bowl plus garlic to pot.

40: Put lid on pot and set temperature to maintain a simmer.

41: Time for clean-up, preparing other items, or non-cooking activities.

83: Remove lid from pot and turn over all chicken pieces. Replace lid.

84: More free time.

128: Remove pot from stovetop. Allow to cool.
    Set timer for 40 minutes.

168: Store in refrigerator for reheating on Tuesday.

VARIATIONS

Replace the wine with wine vinegar (in the coq au vin — not for drinking), and add a can of tomatoes instead of the mushrooms and bacon. (That *vinegar* can successfully replace the wine is another argument against specifying the use of Chambertin.)

Add 25 g of dried mushrooms, after soaking for 15 minutes in a jar in 125 ml of hot water. Add the liquid in place of half of the wine.

The chicken can be replaced by guinea fowl or pheasant. Despite the reputation (and higher cost) of pheasant, the results are not significantly different.

More radically, the chicken can be replaced with beef to produce boeuf bourguignon. Ask your butcher for the most suitable cuts of meat. As with coq au vin, there are numerous more complex recipes which are interesting to attempt, assuming you want to spend time and cognitive resources on research, modification of shopping lists, and adjusting your schedule, in exchange for a probably small improvement in the result.

COMMON RESOURCE MAINTENANCE: POTATO AND LEEK SOUP

The deliciousness of this soup is partly due to the unnamed ingredient — bacon, a flavor enhancer so flexible that Americans use it in bourbon and ice-cream. However, it can be deleted and the chicken stock replaced by vegetable stock or water for a healthier vegetarian[1] option.

The quantity is sufficient for eight serves and is readily scaled up; hence, freeze for future Mondays and / or use for weekday lunches.

COMMON RESOURCES

4 cups chicken stock
2 cloves garlic
400 g potatoes

RECIPE-SPECIFIC INGREDIENTS

200 g bacon, cut 1 cm thick
3 medium leeks

EQUIPMENT

Enameled cast-iron pot

PROCESS

Time: 2 1/2 hours — minimal work after first 25 minutes.

Timing of this recipe is non-critical. If component preparation takes extra time (possibly due to

---

[1] Healthier due to the deletion of bacon rather than the change in stock.

scaling up), the frying times can be increased without adverse effect.

0:    Cut bacon into 1 cm cubes.

5:    Heat oil in pot on burner / hotplate at 70% of maximum temperature.

6:    Add bacon to pot.

Time-share bacon cooking (stir for 5 seconds every 2 minutes) with leek and garlic preparation. Tear off tough outer leaves of leek and cut off root. Beginning at root end (whitest), cut each leek into 5–7 cm slices. Stop when leek becomes noticeably tough and discard remainder. Repeat for all leeks. Peel garlic and cut into tiny pieces (60 seconds chopping).

13:    Add leeks and garlic to pot, and stir with wooden spoon. Time-share leek and bacon cooking (stir for 5 seconds every 2 minutes) with potato preparation. Peel potato(es) and cut into 1 cm cubes.

17:    Add potatoes to pot. Stir with wooden spoon for 5 seconds every 2 minutes.

25:    Add stock to pot and stir. Increase heat to maximum. When fluid boils, lower temperature to maintain simmer.

120: Remove soup from heat and allow to cool.

150: Divide soup into meal-sized portions (if you are considering using it for lunches, make single-person portions). Freeze all but tomorrow night's meal, which can be stored in the refrigerator.

WINTER MONDAY:

Potato and Leek Soup

After the preparatory work of Sunday, today's work is trivial and could even be delegated to a competent household member.

I did not design the Standardized Meal System to minimize cooking time. I enjoy cooking and eating the results. But if you don't enjoy cooking or need to devote the time to more important tasks (e.g. care of a household member or solving the Riemann hypothesis), the Standardized Meal System is the perfect platform for minimizing cooking time. Recipes can be selected from books which focus on speed of preparation or meals which can be made in huge quantities and frozen. Any bulk preparation should probably be outsourced, as there is a risk that an inexperienced cook working with large quantities of ingredients while distracted by the Riemann hypothesis would create a disaster.

(It would be an incredible endorsement of the Standardized Meal System if the solver of the Riemann hypothesis credited it either for providing the necessary time or, in the manner in which I use it, encouraging creative thinking during the cooking process.)

VARIATION

Serve the soup with bread: this will require an extra shopping trip (possibly by another household member) to ensure freshness. Alternatively, purchase a bread-making machine.

Jerusalem Artichoke Soup; Gougères (Cheese Puffs); Coq au Vin with Roasted Broccoli

Wine: pinot noir (Burgundy is the traditional accompaniment to both coq au vin and gougères — mentioning this will increase the intimidation factor of the meal, at least on the first occasion for each set of guests).

My recipes for guest night are for four people, based on two couples: hosts and guests. Obviously, not everyone is in a couple, but some other configurations will also lead to a total of four. I recommend this as a maximum for productive conversation. I find it difficult to reduce my own contribution to 25%[1] and it is impractical to properly develop an argument with less time. In larger groups, people are reluctant to advance an unpopular position for (well-founded) fear of being overwhelmed by the majority.

Socially, it is hard to "get to know" people in large groups, due to the rapidly increasing number of binary interactions (n [n–1] / 2). A dinner "party" for eight entails 8 x 7 / 2 = 28 different pairings, and thus begins to suffer from all the problems of an actual party.

Also, the more people you invite, the more quickly you will run out of potential invitees, and the more often they will experience the same meal, and possibly become less impressed with your expertise as a chef.

In winter, it is psychologically appropriate to welcome guests with soup and / or a "warming" drink. These can

[1] Rosie measured this in order to support her hypothesis that I made a greater contribution to conversation than others.

be combined by adding 1 tablespoon of oloroso sherry or Verdelho Madeira to each serving of the soup, immediately prior to giving it to the guest.

The only non-trivial components of this meal are the gougères (recipe from Patricia Wells, with minor modifications) and broccoli. If under time pressure (or any form of pressure) they can be readily eliminated, and the gruyere served with other Common Resource cheese as a separate course after the chicken.

COMMON RESOURCES: GOUGÈRES

These quantities, except for the cheese, are exact (recommended tolerance 5%).

1/2 tsp salt

120 g unsalted butter

120 g flour

4 eggs

160 g gruyere cheese (parmesan, which you will have on hand for the broccoli, and conventional "cheddar" cheese produce acceptable results)

COMMON RESOURCES: RICE

350 g rice of your preferred variety (as it is guest night, consider an exotic variety)

COMMON RESOURCES: ROASTED BROCCOLI

Parmesan cheese

RECIPE-SPECIFIC INGREDIENTS: ROASTED BROCCOLI

350 g broccoli or 300 g broccolini

EQUIPMENT

Rice cooker with plastic ladle

Baking dish

Sieve

Bowl

Electric mixer

Grater

Enameled cast-iron pot

Cups or small bowls for serving small quantities of soup

Sheet of baking paper or silicone baking mat

PROCESS

Time: approximately 40 minutes work over an elapsed time dictated by personal schedule (preparation) and guest requirements (serving).

Before guests arrive:

Prepare broccoli: break into individual "florets" — length approximately 8 cm — and discard the remainder of central stem (not necessary if using broccolini).

Put broccoli in baking dish with 2 tablespoons of olive oil. Grate 3 tablespoons of parmesan cheese, add to dish, and toss using hands if nobody watching, spoons otherwise.

Don't wash the grater (yet) — it will be required for the gougères.

Prepare gougères mix:

Sift flour into bowl using sieve.

Grate cheese.

Put baking paper / mat on oven tray.

Put salt, butter, and 1 cup of water in a medium saucepan. Place on burner / hotplate on maximum heat and stir with wooden spoon until boiling. Remove from heat and add the sifted flour, rapidly, then beat with spoon until no lumps remain (30 seconds). Reheat at 60% of maximum heat for 40 seconds, while stirring. Transfer contents of medium saucepan to electric mixer bowl. Add eggs and 80% of cheese. Beat at medium speed for 30 seconds.

Use tablespoon to transfer contents of mixer bowl to the baking paper / mat in 8 equal piles with maximum spacing. Distribute remaining cheese equally on top of the piles.

Twenty minutes before anticipated arrival of guests:

1. Heat oven (conventional setting) to 220 degrees.
2. Put Jerusalem artichoke soup on burner / hotplate, ready to reheat.
3. Put coq au vin (in enameled cast-iron pot, lid on) on burner / hotplate, ready to reheat.

On arrival of guests (burst of impressive activity):

Turn on burner / hotplate to 50% of maximum to reheat Jerusalem artichoke soup.

Put oven tray and contents in oven. Set timer for 24 minutes.

Initiate cooking of rice.

When soup reaches boiling point, allow to boil for 15 seconds, then turn off burner / hotplate, and divide into cups or bowls.

Timer sounds: begin reheating coq au vin at 50% of maximum temperature.

Remove gougères from oven.

Reduce oven temperature to 180 degrees and put baking dish with broccoli in oven. Set timer for 25 minutes.

Serve gougères.

Check coq au vin every 10 minutes and stir. When it reaches boiling point (typically 20 minutes), allow to boil for 15 seconds, then reduce heat to simmer.

When timer sounds, serve coq au vin with broccoli and rice.

VARIATIONS

Sprinkle smoked paprika on top of the gougères.

Serve prosciutto or marinated peppers with the gougères.

Omit the oloroso sherry and grate fresh truffle on the soup. This variant was prompted by Gene, who arrived one evening with a single black truffle, observing that it was cheaper than the bottle of Chambertin I had requested in response to his question "Can I bring anything?" If you want to try exotic ingredients such as caviar and truffles — and Burgundy — it is vastly cheaper to do so at home and even more so if the guests are paying. We collectively rated the truffle 8.7 / 10 for aroma and 3.3 / 10 for flavor.

Lentil Stew; Chocolates

When I was a university student, living in Melbourne away from my family in Shepparton (a situation with both positive and negative features), I lived in a share(d) house. Responsibility for meals was rostered and I quickly settled on a standard solution, which was extremely cheap and acceptable to all household members, including a vegan[1]. It can be made entirely from Common Resources, if you use a can of tomatoes instead of the fresh tomato and capsicum.

I have continued to cook this meal. It is not as good as lobster salad with mango and avocado (refer Summer Tuesday) but not *significantly* inferior, and if I was close to solving the Riemann hypothesis or finding a cure for cancer, and in financial difficulty, I would be happy to eat it every night.

COMMON RESOURCES

1 brown onion

2 cloves of garlic

1 tbsp smoked sweet or hot paprika (critical ingredient)

1 bay leaf

1 small potato

1 carrot

125 g (approx. 3/4 cup) dried brown or green lentils[2]

---

[1] Since I had one "bad date" with a vegan, I (probably unreasonably) excluded vegans from the Wife Project. This vegan was an extremely nice person who was attempting to live an ethical life, *the* major challenge for all reasonable people.

[2] Other lentil varieties can be used but require careful timing to avoid disintegration into dhal texture.

RECIPE-SPECIFIC INGREDIENTS

1 green capsicum
1 conventional tomato or 10 cherry tomatoes

EQUIPMENT

Sieve
Enameled cast-iron pot

PROCESS

Time: 70 minutes, including 30 minutes unallocated time.

Rinse the lentils in the sieve.

Peel onion, potato, and carrot. Cut capsicum in half and remove core. Chop all vegetables into 1 cm cubes. If using cherry tomatoes, chopping is optional; if using a whole tomato, chop into 1 cm cubes.

Chop garlic into tiny pieces (60 seconds chopping).

Put pot on burner / hotplate and set temperature to 50% of maximum. Add 1 tablespoon of oil, plus vegetables, tomato(es), and garlic.

Cook for 20 minutes. Stir after 10 minutes.

Add the paprika and the bay leaf. Stir for 15 seconds. Add lentils and 2 cups of water, stir, and increase heat to maximum.

When boiling point is reached, adjust heat to maintain simmer.

After 25 minutes, check that lentils are cooked (if not, continue until they are).

Remove bay leaf from pot, then serve.

Chocolates.

VARIATIONS

This dish can be made non-vegan by adding two sausages — I recommend uncooked chorizo — which are fried, grilled, or barbecued, then sliced and added to the stew 10 minutes before serving or served on a separate plate (especially if there is a vegan in the household). Alternatively, use bacon, fried before adding the vegetables. This will change the overall flavor of the dish, but (especially in Dave's opinion) in a positive direction.

In the absence of a vegan, you can use chicken stock instead of water. When I lived in the share(d) house, one of my housemates would add an unmeasured splash of sherry five minutes prior to serving. If you are adding fried sausages, you can deglaze the pan with sherry and add to the stew.

Poppadums; Chicken Curry

If I want an authentic Indian meal, I visit our excellent local Indian restaurant. This principle applies to most exotic (to me) and complex food. At one time, I suggested that we eat Indian cuisine every night, which would enable me to assemble the appropriate base ingredients and acquire the necessary skills, pointing out that almost 18% of the world's population does so. Rosie was unenthusiastic.

However, commercial Indian curry pastes are remarkably palatable. I suggest you experiment with different products and with adding chopped vegetables — spinach, zucchini, broccoli, peas, pre-cooked potato — to the curry, to increase nutritional value. Or replacing the meat with vegetables altogether.

I have specified chicken (seafood is also an option) rather than red meat because of the goal of having only one red-meat meal per week. If you don't observe that rule, or are prepared to make an exception in winter, you can use lamb, beef, pork, goat, or kangaroo.

I recommend poppadums as a starter, primarily because they are so easy and spectacular to cook.

COMMON RESOURCES

Commercial curry paste ("Madras," "Vindaloo," etcetera)
Commercial chutney and pickles (at least a jar of each)
1 brown onion
3/4 cup rice of your preferred variety
1 can tomatoes, 400g (depending on choice of paste)
2 poppadums

RECIPE-SPECIFIC INGREDIENTS

350 g diced chicken (if you have to dice it yourself,
  2 1/2 cm cubes)
150 g baby spinach (or adult spinach, which is now
  harder to find; optional)
1 medium zucchini (optional)

EQUIPMENT

Rice cooker with plastic ladle
Frying pan for poppadums
Enameled cast-iron pot
Bowl

PROCESS

*Time: typically 40 minutes, including significant
unallocated time.*

Put rice and specified quantity of water in rice
cooker and activate.

Cook poppadums according to instructions on
packet — 1 per person. Serve with chutneys and
pickles, and leave these on the table to eat with
the main course.

If the curry recipe does *not* specify onion, I
recommend adding it: peel an onion, chop into
1 cm cubes, heat 1 tablespoon of cooking oil in
pot over 30% of maximum heat, cook onion for
5 minutes, then transfer to a bowl and put back
in the pot after the meat has been browned.

Follow the instructions on the curry-paste jar.

While the initial stages of the cooking are proceeding, cut zucchini into 1 cm discs.
If spinach is large, chop into 4 cm squares[1].

When the liquid and / or tomatoes are added, also add the zucchini and spinach.

Continue with recipe, per jar instructions.

Serve with rice, chutneys, and pickles.

VARIATIONS

Ignore my variations specified in recipe and make exactly according to instructions on jar.

Experiment with increasing the proportion of any individual spice. These will be listed on jar.

Add uncooked peas (frozen are acceptable) to the rice cooker.

Purchase Indian sweets (interesting, delicious, zero work) and serve as dessert.

---

[1] Periodic reminder: *approximately*.

Restaurant Night or Fusilli Pizzaiola

Recommended cocktail: Old Fashioned.

Recommended wine: red, due to pasta.

If you are familiar with authentic Italian cuisine, you will recognize this meal as inauthentic. Pasta is supposed to be served with only a small quantity of sauce, in the same way that "authentic" pizza is not piled high with interesting toppings.

Considering how delicious and popular the alternatives are, I assume that these "rules" arose from the need to be economical with toppings, rather than from an objective assessment of flavor.

My rule for pizza and pasta is "if it tastes good on pizza, it is worth considering as a pasta topping, possibly after further chopping."[1] The reverse is not true.

COMMON RESOURCES

180 g fusilli pasta

1 brown onion

22 black olives (preferably marinated in oil, but brine-marinated olives will work)

90 g (9 cm of typical diameter) hot or mild salami

1 can tomatoes, 400g

3 cloves garlic

1 birds-eye or alternative preferred chili, fresh or reconstituted (optional)

Parmesan cheese

---

[1] I do not recommend sharing this opinion with your risotto consultant — refer Spring Wednesday.

EQUIPMENT

Large pot for boiling pasta
Frying pan
Grater

PROCESS

Time: 25 minutes.

Cut salami into 1 cm cubes and olives in half.

Peel onion and cut into 5 mm cubes.

Peel garlic and cut into tiny pieces
(60 seconds chopping).

Heat 2 tablespoons of olive oil in frying pan
at 40% of maximum heat.

Add chopped onion and garlic to pan, and fry
for 5 minutes.

Add salami, olives, tomatoes, and (optionally)
chili to pan. Stir and cook for 5 minutes.

Cook pasta in pot according to instructions
on packet (add 1 tablespoon of salt when the
water boils if not specified).

Add cooked pasta to frying pan, stir to mix,
and serve.

Put parmesan on table with grater to enable
diners to grate cheese over their pasta
(fresh, zero wastage).

VARIATIONS

Soak 10 g of dried mushrooms in warm water for 15 minutes and add with the tomatoes.

As this is a Friday meal, it is designed to be made entirely from Common Resources. But if I was planning it in advance, I would include a chopped zucchini (1 1/2 cm cubes) and 200 g of fresh mushrooms (1 cm cubes), which I would fry in the pan for 5 minutes after the onion-and-garlic-frying step. This information is worth sharing with household members. Illustrative text from Rosie:

> *I'm not up to going out tonight. I'll grab mushrooms and zucchini at the supermarket on the way home so we can have some VEGETABLES. Open that chianti.*

Rosie only knew which ingredients and wine were required because of the predictability of the Standardized Meal System. (Mushrooms are fungi, not vegetables, but are nutritionally similar.)

Collaborators

It is not possible to copyright a recipe (chefs should consider employing university lawyers). Those in this book have diverse origins; if I have seen further, it is only because I was (metaphorically) standing on the shoulders of giants[1], whom I have acknowledged where I am aware of them, or because I have different eyes (also metaphorically). I am prepared to make a cocktail for any chef whose recipe I have adapted.

Prior to commencing this project, I asked several associates to record their actual dinners for one week. The results were surprising, even to me, and highlighted the value of the Standardized Meal System. Several respondents volunteered to join my team of recipe testers. I had cooked the meals multiple times, but had not verified that the documentation was usable by others. My testers were incredible, but no blame should accrue to them or to me in the event of meal inedibility, sickness, injury, or death. If in doubt, seek your own professional advice.

Survey respondents and recipe testers were (alphabetically, couples concatenated): Anne Buist and Graeme Simsion, Tania Chandler, Peter Dawson and Karin Whitehead, Robert Eames and Wendy Geraghty, Alaina Gougoulis, Irina Goundortseva,

---

[1] Excellent quote used by Isaac Newton. It is important to acknowledge that our achievements are built on those of others. When his theory of relativity supplanted Newton's laws, Albert Einstein wrote, "Forgive me, Newton..." I was moved to tears by this information.

Greg Jones, Cathie and David Lange, Lynette Leber and Rod Miller and the carers at the MS Society of Victoria (Williamstown), Duncan Macdougall and Dominique Simsion, Patti Patcha, Rebecca Peniston-Bird, Michèle and Robert Sachs, Imogen Stubbs, Sue and Chris Waddell, Geri and Pete Walsh, and Janifer and Terry Willis.

This book was written as a result of *extreme pressure* from Michael Heyward, CEO of Text Publishing, with specific expertise from David Winter (editor), Chong Weng-Ho, Jessica Horrocks, and Imogen Stubbs (design and production).

Obviously, given the vast number of recipe books available, written by chefs far more qualified than me, I needed to rely on experts in book marketing, sales, and publicity to convince buyers of the advantages of the Standardized Meal System. Fortunately, the incredible team of Shalini Kunahlan, Kate Lloyd, Patti Patcha, and Jane Watkins was assigned to the task. Anne Beilby and Khadija Caffoor have ensured that the previous *Rosie* books have been translated into over forty languages, and I expect them to have similar success with this book.

Now I can return to the search for a cure for cancer.

Shopping and Equipment

Download user-modifiable shopping lists to help you source ingredients for the Standardized Meal System, and a user-modifiable equipment list: **bit.ly/TillmanMealSystem**

Other books featuring Professor Don Tillman available from Text Publishing: